GUT INSTINCT

BASED ON A TRUE STORY

HANNAH McNAMARA

Black Rose Writing | Texas

ISBN: 978-1-68513-654-3
LIBRARY OF CONGRESS CONTROL NUMBER: 2025935425
PUBLISHED BY BLACK ROSE WRITING
www.blackrosewriting.com

Printed in the United States of America
Suggested Retail Price (SRP) $18.95

Gut Instinct is printed in Chaparral Pro

*As a planet-friendly publisher, Black Rose Writing does its best to eliminate unnecessary waste to reduce paper usage and energy costs, while never compromising the reading experience. As a result, the final word count vs. page count may not meet common expectations.

Praise for
GUT INSTINCT

"When your instincts are wrong, can you ever trust them again? Only if you want to live..."
–Cam Torrens, award-winning author of the *Tyler Zahn* suspense series

"*Gut Instinct's* smooth prose and quick pace will keep you riveted to Hannah McNamara's YA page-turner from page one. Your heart will pound alongside Willow Carter's, as she struggles to keep herself and her family safe when their family beach vacation goes awry. This book is for anyone who has ever had to trust their deepest instincts while facing their deepest fears."
–Suzanne Akerman, author of *The Deliverers*

"When the man camping next door gives Willow, Ella, and the dog the creeps, they listen to their instincts and remain alert. *Gut Instinct* is a realistic and chilling story about a near tragedy."
–Lena Gibson, award-winning author of *The Love and Survival* series

"A cautionary tale of danger in sheep's clothing. When alarm bells ring in the face of a smiling stranger, it could be time to trust yourself."
–Sarah Nakawatase, author of *Dormant Diversion*

To everyone out there who has ever had a gut instinct about something or someone, this is your encouragement to do one thing: trust it. Also, to Max, for being the best protector I could ever ask for.

GUT
INSTINCT

CHAPTER 1

Someone was watching me.

The itchy, scalp-tingling sensation trickled uncomfortably through my body, and I whipped my head around to peer through the trees. From high in the crook of two branches, I balanced precariously, tilting my head to stare into the public beach parking lot.

A few scattered, empty picnic tables sat in the lonely lot, along with a handful of cars. The dune grass around the lot swayed gently in the wind, but I could barely tell through my tree-blocked view. The feeling of someone watching me faded when it was clear no one occupied the tables or the property. The surrounding canopy of trees was vacant except for petite, teenage me. I closed my eyes and placed my head back against the trunk of the tree. The smell of Mom's cooking wafted from our campsite just a short distance away, leaving a warm feeling in my chest.

There it was again.

A prickle began at the base of my neck, percolating down my spine and into my head. Goosebumps appeared on my arms and legs and I quickly tried to rub them away. I turned my head toward the parking lot again.

A man sat at a picnic table, watching me.

Five Years Later

"Just a few more things," Dad muttered, picking up his fishing gear and placing it in the back of our Ford Expedition. I noticed the perspiration dripping from his forehead and neck as I wiped my own forehead, feeling the salty warmth sticking to my hand. I carefully lifted my duffel bag and arranged it into the back of the car, glancing quickly into the garage to see how much baggage was left. Mom appeared at the door leading into the house, beaming as she wiped her hands on her apron.

"Food is all prepared and packed into the cooler! I think that's the last thing that needs to go in the car, and then we can hit the road!" she said.

"I highly doubt that's all we have left to put in the car," Dad whispered to himself.

This was how it usually went before a trip in my family—it started out pleasant as we began loading the car, turned tense as we got more anxious to leave, then everyone became impatient and snappy as we gathered the last few things before departing. I sighed and wiped my hand across my forehead again, silently willing the sweat to stop pouring down my face. A small clatter echoed in the garage, and I looked up to see Dad hoisting one of our many tents up onto the higher shelf after it had fallen down at his feet. After settling it back on the top shelf, Dad's eyes roamed around the garage, doing his typical sweep to check we had everything we needed for the short camping trip. Soft fur brushed against my calf, and I turned my gaze down to see Coach panting at my feet. His warm brown eyes stared happily into mine.

"Just a few more minutes, Coach," I murmured, bending to place my face against his, breathing in his scent before pulling back and continuing to load the car.

Every year for the last several years, my family and my best friend's family planned to meet in Westport, Washington, for an annual camping trip. I had known my best friend, Ella, since childhood. We grew up just minutes from each other, but her family moved to another state a few years ago. This camping trip was the only time we spent together each year.

Dad finally deemed the car ready with all our bags and food packed inside, and Mom, Coach, and I piled in and adjusted ourselves for the trip. I popped one earbud in and laid my head on my pillow against the car window. I glimpsed into the sky, where the hot August sun was beating down on us. Although it was a sunny seventy-five outside, Dad liked to keep the Ford cold during longer drives. He always claimed his "body ran hot." Consequently, on every car ride that lasted longer than an hour, Mom and I wore warmer clothes and even sometimes snuggled in a blanket.

Coach settled his head onto my lap and let out a dramatic sigh.

"Was that Coach that made that noise?" Mom asked, stifling a laugh.

"Yeah, he's clearly feeling a little tired," I said, petting the top of his head. A five-year-old Australian Shepherd, I couldn't imagine our family without him.

"Coach? Really? He doesn't even know the *word* 'tired,'" Mom said, reaching back to scratch Coach's leg.

The rest of the three-hour drive went by smoothly, with just one break. Mom requested we stop to get coffees.

"Evelyn, do you really need another one? What are we teaching our seventeen-year-old daughter by consuming so much caffeine?" Dad had protested. Mom fixed him with a scowl so steely it had *my* skin crawling.

"Dad, seriously? I think you know my caffeine addiction started years ago, and it's not stopping anytime soon," I said matter-of-factly. After about thirty seconds of the death glare from Mom, Dad gave in and pulled into the nearest Starbucks.

Back on the road, I stared out the windows, watching intently as the buildings became more sparse, until eventually we were surrounded by mostly dried grass and trees. Westport was a small beach town with one big road going down the center of it and a handful of side roads and neighborhoods encompassing it. I always enjoyed the small-town feel of it. It made me feel safe. The only time it hadn't was *that* summer. The summer I lost my parents' trust quicker than I ever could have imagined.

We pulled into the campgrounds, stopping at the ranger kiosk to check in. Dad jumped out and told us to stay put as he confirmed our campsite number with the ticket booth worker. I pulled my phone out and glanced at the screen, which had just lit up with a text.

"Mom, Ella says they won't arrive for another couple of hours. We left way ahead of them," I explained as I read the text from my best friend.

Ella, her parents, Larry and Amy, and her younger eight-year-old sister, Margot, were all attending the camping trip this year. Every so often, Larry had to miss the camping trip due to work. I was glad this year they would all be here. It made things feel more exciting when everyone was present. I texted Ella, *Hurry up and get here*. The driver's door to the Ford swung open, and Dad climbed back into his seat.

"Okay, we're all set. We're in campsite 232. The Grishams are in 234, right next to us, so you can let Ella know they're stuck with us," Dad said to me, laughing at his own joke while giving Mom a wink. He put the car into drive again, slowly inching his way around the ticket booth and entering the campground. I glanced forward through the front windshield, and a tingle of excitement ran down my spine. I loved everything about staying at this campground every August—the location, the greenery, the ocean. It had been a tradition to come here since I was five years old, so I could walk through this campground with my eyes closed and still know every bump in the road and every hill in the sand. Dad maneuvered the Ford through the first loop of the campground—the one farthest from the ocean.

"Are you excited about taking your senior photos tonight?" Mom's voice cut through my thoughts.

"Yes, but I'll be more excited once Ella is here," I replied, feeling the car jostle up and down through the bumps in the road. I sunk my hand into Coach's thick fur around his neck, scratching him in one of his favorite spots. The dog glanced up at me and panted, his eyes squinted and happy. Dad looked at both sides of the road before driving across it and into the second loop of the campground.

Finally, I thought.

I rolled my window down and breathed in the salty ocean air as we made our way around the loop. The ocean wasn't directly visible from where we were, but it was just a short walking distance away. Close enough to smell the salt and hear the waves. Coach loved the smells and sounds of the ocean, sticking his black fluffy head out the window next to mine and pointing his nose in the air.

"Nick, this site is ours," Mom said, pointing toward our usual campsite.

It was, first and foremost, empty. It had the normal metal fire pit drilled into the soft soil, along with a barren wooden picnic table a few feet away. But my focus lay right behind our campsite—the forest.

Hundreds of large lodgepole pine trees surrounded us, their tops creating a forested canopy under which various dune grass species grew from the forest floor. The grasses were tall enough to be waist-high on most people, and they could easily slice your legs up if you went running through them.

The forest had always intrigued me. My parents hadn't allowed me to explore it alone until I was about eleven, and even then, they planted a walkie-talkie in my hand and told me to call them if I got lost. They had good reason to be worried, as the forest was immensely long, stretching on for acres behind all the campsites. It wasn't deep width-wise, and people often hiked through it to get to the beach, which sat about a quarter of a mile on the other side of the green belt. Despite the razor-sharp dune grass and lack of light due to the thick pines, there was something special about being in the forest. I liked the solitude, the way I could climb a tree and feel the wind whip strands of my braided hair free. I relished in discovering every nook, cranny, and hiding spot the tall grass and bushy pines had to offer. I loved exploring in it for hours and getting lost, only to pop my head up and realize I was on the other side of our loop and was peering into someone else's campsite.

These thoughts were racing through my head just as my phone pinged. I startled and looked down at the bright screen, seeing Ella's name with a message underneath that read, *If I told Dad to hurry his butt up, like you said, he would go even slower. The map says we'll be there in an hour and a half. Don't go exploring the Thicket without me.* I laughed as I read the name Ella and I had given the forest three years ago, a memory flashing through my mind.

"Margot, how about you, Willow, and I play hide-and-seek?" Ella's voice rang through the forest, bouncing off the trees.

I glanced down to where my best friend sat below me on a thick branch, dangling her feet. My eyes watered from stifling a laugh as Margot tried for the sixth time to pull herself higher into the tree across from Ella and me. Her tiny five-year-old hand could barely reach the branch above her, and she certainly did not have enough strength to hoist herself up more. Margot grunted and dropped her arms back down, clearly frustrated she couldn't climb higher.

"Fine, but you have to count first, and Willow and I will hide," Margot said, crossing her arms. Ella peered up at me to where I perched, which was a few branches above her, and sighed.

"Okay, but whoever climbs down last has to be the next one to count!" she exclaimed, getting to her feet and scurrying to descend.

My heart raced as I shouted, "Hey, that's not fair! I'm higher than everyone! And I have to wait for your scrawny butt to get down before I can even go!" I started to turn my back and place my feet onto the bark, digging my toes in to steady myself.

"Exactly!" Both Ella and Margot giggled as they landed on the forest floor with a thump.

I made my way down the pine tree, holding onto different branches for support. I finally landed beside them with a similar thump when my shoes hit the soil.

"I could explore for days. It feels so magical here. There must be a hundred trees to climb," I spoke softly, touching some nearby moss that grew on the tree bark.

"Yeah, we should try to climb at least ten different trees each camping trip!" Margot said excitedly. Ella and I nodded our heads in agreement.

"You know, we should give this place a name. We come in here so often, and 'the forest' sounds lame and doesn't even do it justice," Ella said, looking up at the pine needle canopy. "Let's call it 'the Thicket.' That sounds way cooler!"

I followed her line of sight up to treetops, admiring the way the sun filtered in through the gaps. After a few seconds of silence, I nodded.

"I like it. 'The Thicket.' Sounds intense," I said. I could see Margot's head bobbing out of the corner of my eye.

"Wait, Margot, it's time for hide-and-seek! Let's go hide!" I grabbed the five-year-old's sweaty hand in mine and started racing through the grass, only wincing slightly as I felt the blades cut through my skin. I could hear Ella's counting get quieter as Margot and I hiked farther into the Thicket, eventually crouching behind a large bush entangled with a stocky pine tree. Margot's damp hand was still in mine, and I felt her give a light squeeze as we barely deciphered Ella's voice saying, "Three...two...one..."

"Willow! Get out of the car! We need help unpacking!" Dad's voice rang through my head, causing the memory to fade away in an instant. My parents were both grabbing boxes out of the car and placing them onto the wooden picnic table.

Mom gave me an exasperated look through the car window. "You zoned out there for a second. Coach is about ready to leap over your lap and bust through the car door," she said, throwing her hands up.

"Sorry, I was just remembering something." I pulled the door handle and let Coach jump out. "Let me come help."

I wiped the hair out of my face as I climbed out after Coach, fixing my eyes on the trees beyond the campsite.

"Oh no, no, no. Don't even think about exploring the Thicket until you help us unpack." Mom's death glare entered my vision, blocking the trees. As my hazel-hued eyes met her chocolate brown ones, I detected a bit of humor in her gaze.

"Seems like everyone has started to use the forest's official name now. It's grown on you, hasn't it?" I smirked, walking past her to grab the camp chairs in the trunk.

My peripheral vision caught a glimpse of movement, and I turned to see a man who appeared to be in his thirties, one campsite over from ours, on the other side of the Grisham's site. A blue Coleman tent occupied his campsite, along with a beat-up black

Camry. He sat in a royal blue camping chair that matched the color of his tent. I quickly noted that he didn't have a cooler sitting out, or rather, anything sitting out, other than the tent, chair, and his car. Nothing was on his picnic table except an empty bag of Lay's sour cream and onion chips.

I swallowed and averted my eyes, fear creeping through my veins inexplicably and my stomach plummeting. I quickly got the sense that something about this man was...*off*. It was one of those gut instincts, and from just one glance at him, my whole body screamed that something was wrong. My hands felt clammy as I tried to keep my grip on the box of bug spray and sunscreen, carefully bringing it to the table. Allowing my eyes to roam over the man's campsite again, I was surprised to realize he looked very unremarkable. Tousled light brown hair fell well above his eyes, contrasting his dark eyes. He couldn't have been much taller than five foot ten inches.

Maybe he just arrived and hasn't unpacked much, I thought to myself.

The troubled feeling in my stomach didn't go away, though. Walking back to the open trunk of the Ford, I tapped Mom on the shoulder and motioned for her to stroll with me to the passenger side, where we were out of the man's sight. Giving me a confused and slightly concerned look, she reluctantly followed.

"What is it? You look like you've seen a ghost," she murmured, placing her hands on her hips.

"Did you see that guy? The one who's one campsite over from us?" I whispered urgently, nodding my head toward the direction of his campsite.

"I mean, I suppose I glanced over at him. Why?" she asked, tilting her head.

"He gives me a bad vibe. I don't know what it is. He looks harmless, but I had a weird feeling when I first saw him. I think we should keep an eye on him," I said quietly, averting my eyes to the ground in slight embarrassment. The last time I tried to warn her about someone I thought was sketchy, it hadn't exactly turned out well.

Mom threw her head back and let out a small laugh. My eyes crinkled in skepticism, and I snuck another peek at his campsite.

"Willow, seriously? You're being dramatic. He looks like a guy who would give out free samples at Costco. Harmless, like you said. Now come on, we need to put the tent up," she said the last bit as she turned away from me, heading toward the even patch of ground where Dad had laid the tent.

Frustrated, I let out a groan and pressed the heels of my palms against my eyes. She was probably right. He wasn't dangerous, but she didn't need to be so dismissive about it. I yanked my phone out of my pocket to shoot a quick text to Ella.

Hey, there's a weird guy camping on one side of you guys. We're on your other side, so you're sandwiched between us and the weirdo. Wanted to give you a heads up.

I clicked send and shoved the device back in my pocket. Mom and Dad began picking the poles up and placing them through the flaps on the tent. I grabbed the last plastic pole and positioned it to run across the top of the tent, securing it into the ground on each side. Within minutes, the large, olive green tent was up and stable with the stakes hammered into the dirt. Dad's sweaty arm swung up in the air, and I clapped my hand against his, completing the high-five.

"I swear you get faster at setting that up every year," he said, his smile widening. I grinned back, thinking about the past years when I was too young to even understand how a tent worked.

"Wait, Dad?"

"Yeah, honey, what's up?" A ray of sun shone directly into Dad's eyes, and he lifted his hand up to block it.

"I think that guy in the campsite next to the Grisham's is weird. I got a bad feeling from him. Just thought I'd tell you." I peered up at his jade green eyes, which were still glinting from the sunlight peeking through Dad's fingers, and tried to decipher if he would take me seriously or not.

Dad's gaze flitted briefly to where the man was sitting in his campsite before he let out a deep sigh. "Honey, let's not have another bad experience like a few years ago. There's nothing we can do about him camping there. Just ignore him, okay?" he said, reaching out with his other hand to pat my shoulder.

I was about to elaborate on the unusual gut feeling I had when I felt my pocket buzz. I dug my phone out, seeing Ella's name on the screen.

You've watched too many episodes of Forensic Files. But I'll let you know if I think he's weird once I see him. BTW- we're ten minutes away!

Relief washed over me. At least Ella hadn't dismissed me as much as my parents had and was willing to assess him herself. I stole a look at the man again and found the uncomfortable tingle crawling back through my veins. The firepit in front of him was a heap of gray ashes and burnt wood, but he stared intensely at it anyway.

Twelve minutes of unpacking, setting up the camp kitchen, and me warily watching the creepy man passed by until I heard the slow familiar rumble of the Grisham's Silver GMC Acadia. I whipped my head up from where I was unraveling a smaller second tent for Ella and myself and tucked a few loose strands of brown hair behind my ear. My braids never lasted long, even though I had lengthy, wavy hair that went nearly all the way down my back. Small strands always came loose after just a couple of hours, and it was a pain to deal with. Pushing myself up from my knees, I eagerly watched as the Acadia backed into the campsite right between ours and the lone man. A few seconds later, the back door swung open forcibly, and Margot and Ella tumbled out in excitement.

Before I knew it, my feet were moving swiftly across the solid earth, and I reached my friends in a few strides and pulled both of them into a tight embrace.

"You're here!" I exclaimed.

Living in a different state than my best friend was hard. After eighth grade, her dad, Larry, received a job offer in Coeur d'Alene, Idaho, and the Grishams had packed up and moved before Ella and I could start high school together. We went from talking face-to-face daily to texting and occasionally FaceTiming. Even though Idaho bordered Washington, it felt like Ella was on another planet sometimes.

"We're here!" Margot said excitedly. Her freckled face looked no different than last year, but her dirty blonde hair had grown a few inches past her shoulders.

"You're almost as tall as me now." I looked her up-and-down and laughed. Margot had always been a little tall for her age, but it seemed her gangly limbs had stretched even more since the last time I saw her. My gaze shifted to Ella, who was fixated on something behind her. I followed the direction she was facing slowly, realizing she was staring directly at the guy camped next to her, who still sat idly in his blue camping chair.

"You're right," she whispered. "He is creepy."

I let out a nervous laugh, trying to break the uncomfortable feeling tangling itself into my stomach.

"Come on, let's forget about him. Besides, I need you to help me set up the tent we're sleeping in." I tugged at Ella's hand, urging her to break her stare.

She reluctantly rotated her head back to me and shivered. "Fine, but we're putting our tent on your parent's campsite. The farthest we can get from that guy," she said, pointing her thumb back.

"I wish Mom and Dad would let me sleep in your guys' tent. They say I'm still too young," Margot protested crossly, rolling her eyes.

I looped my right arm through hers and my left arm through Ella's before saying, "Maybe next year. Now let's set up this tent!"

"You didn't really think you could just waltz off without a hug, did you?" Amy's voice rang out just as I started to march off with Margot and Ella.

I let go of my friends' arms before racing back to their car, where Amy was shaking her curly-haired head, her hands on her hips.

"Hi, Amy. I missed you," I said as she pulled me in for a hug. Larry opened the driver's door and climbed out, giving me a curt nod. "Hey, Willow. Good to see you."

I dipped my chin and smiled. "Nice to see you too, Larry."

Larry had always been a quiet guy. He was a shorter man, standing at about five foot eight inches, but he was burly and looked like he could squash someone like a grape. What he lacked in height, he made up for in muscular stature. Larry usually came off as "all business" when he conversed with people, choosing to discuss more formal things and not excelling much at small talk. Contrastingly, Amy could talk anyone's ear off for hours if they let her. She was vibrant and exuberant, but it wasn't a good idea to make her upset or irritated. Amy could yell someone's ear off just as much as she could talk it off, and I was not envious of Ella or Margot in that regard.

"Amy, Larry, so glad you guys are here!" Mom rushed from behind me, pulling Amy in for a hug while Dad shook Larry's hand.

I spun around, knowing this was my moment to escape and spend time with Margot and Ella. Watching the sisters setting the tent up, I couldn't help but smile as their soft laughter resounded through the lively campsite. My parents, Larry, and Amy leisurely moved their conversation to the picnic table, where I could barely detect Dad telling Larry about the new lantern he purchased for this trip.

With the ocean just out of view, anyone with normal hearing could easily listen to what I'm sure were loud, crashing waves. I was born deaf in one ear, so it had always been harder for me to enjoy various sounds. I didn't take any noise my good ear picked up for granted when we camped here. If I stopped and listened past my own campsite, I could just barely hear ocean waves colliding, sometimes followed by an occasional dog barking. Fire crackling, food cooking, people laughing. At night, I sometimes made out hushed conversation or singing around campfires. I closed my eyes and breathed in deeply, allowing my ears to pick up whatever sounds they could. Sometimes, I had to truly focus on hearing certain things to hear them at all. I often turned my head toward particular sounds to concentrate on them better. But now, as I listened to Ella playfully yell Coach's name and Mom chuckle at something Amy said, I felt a rush of happiness and relief. A strong feeling of love and warmth infused my whole being. Smiling, I opened my eyes, but the feeling of joy in my chest quickly vanished as the strange man camping next to the Grishams walked straight into our campsite.

CHAPTER 2

"Hey, everyone," the man announced as he crossed the invisible boundary between the Grisham's campsite and his. "Just wanted to introduce myself. My name is Christian. I'm camping right over there." He pointed a finger back toward his site and smiled.

"Anyway, I came over to ask if you'd keep an eye on my campsite and my stuff while I drive into town. I need to buy some food." He continued talking, even though nobody had moved since he had strolled over. Dad finally stood up from the picnic table and shoved his hands into his pockets. For a moment, I thought he would tell the guy to get the hell away from us.

But instead, Dad said, "Sure, we can do that. And I'm Nicholas, or Nick. This is my wife, Evelyn." He placed his hand gently on Mom's back as she also got up from the table.

Larry and Amy introduced themselves to Christian as well, and then Mom looked at me expectantly. My heart was palpitating, which was silly, since what Christian asked of us was completely normal. I guess my body hadn't shaken off the gut feeling yet.

"I'm Willow," I said slowly, forcing my eyes to meet Christian's. I tried to detect any malice or evil in them, but his eyes were strangely blank. The deep brown color of his irises was so dark it was nearly black, blending in with his pupils and giving him a permanently creepy stare. I barely heard Ella and Margot tell Christian their names through the roaring thoughts in my head telling me this guy was dangerous. I scoffed at myself.

Calm down. You're being dramatic.

Mom's earlier words echoed through my head and I wondered if she was right. This man had done *nothing* to prove he was weird or unsafe. It was simply a feeling I had. Maybe Ella was also right—I've watched too many episodes of Forensic Files.

"Well, it was nice meeting you guys. I'll be back shortly. Thanks for watching my stuff." Christian held up a hand in farewell. His black Camry rumbled as the engine started, leaving a small cloud of dust behind as he drove off. I felt a light squeeze on my left hand, Ella appearing at my side.

"I wonder why he asked us to watch his stuff when all he left behind was his tent and camping chair," she said softly.

"Maybe he has a million dollars in his tent," I joked.

"Maybe he's hiding a child in there!" Margot burst out. Ella shoved her sister's shoulder in annoyance.

"Stop being stupid. He seemed somewhat normal. We should give him the benefit of the doubt," Ella retorted, crossing her arms in defiance.

She was right, I realized. I was raised to be strong, independent, and smart. I knew how to protect myself, and I was surrounded by tons of other people. The intrusive thoughts about Christian needed to end now.

•   •   •   •   •

A couple hours later, we designated my parents' campsite to be the main "campfire" spot, which now contained seven different camp chairs placed haphazardly in a circle around the firepit. The Grisham's site was appointed as the cooking station, where both moms would prepare the food each day with their matching camp kitchens. Earlier, Ella and I shoved two picnic tables together to create one long dining area in the middle of my parents' site and the Grisham's. A hammock was tied between two trees near the Thicket.

Larry and Amy's bright red tent, which would also house Margot, sat on their own site in the most level patch of ground they could find. Unfortunately, the spot they chose was just about ten feet from Christian's tent. The olive green tent would lodge my parents, placed on the other side of Larry and Amy's.

Ella and I would sleep in our separate tent, thankfully being the farthest from Christian's. Just as everyone was standing back and admiring the handiwork of the last two hours, Christian's black Camry pulled into his spot.

"He was gone for two hours. That's a long grocery run," Mom remarked.

Coach nudged my hand with his wet nose, pushing his forehead underneath my palm for pets. Swinging his door open, Christian exited the car, holding a singular plastic bag in his hand. He jogged over to us, thanking us for watching his stuff. Coach's body shifted slightly beneath my hand as the man approached my parents. I glanced down, only to hear him growl and bare his teeth at Christian.

"Hey, hey, Coach, it's okay," I whispered softly, kneeling down to be eye-level with him.

"Willow, grab the dog, will you? Sorry about that. He usually doesn't growl at people," Mom said. She widened her eyes at me and motioned toward the dog, looking embarrassed. Christian gave a sidelong look over at me and Coach while I grabbed his collar.

"I know I've already asked a lot of you, but I bought this really nice halibut when I was out, and I was hoping I could store it in your cooler? I forgot mine," Christian said to Dad, still peering at Coach and me through his peripherals. Larry frowned slightly, but kept quiet, allowing Dad to answer.

"Oh, that's fine, I guess." Dad laughed awkwardly and held his hand out for the halibut before continuing, "You know, you may be the only person I've met that didn't bring a cooler with them while camping."

After pausing briefly, Christian spoke up, "Oh, well this was a pretty last-minute trip. I even left my dog behind at my apartment."

"You didn't take your dog camping with you?" Ella's disapproving voice rang out.

Christian's eyes shot over to her. "Nah, he's staying with my roommate. Anyway, thanks for holding on to that halibut for me. I'll grab it from you tomorrow."

He shoved his hands in his pockets, looking a little uncomfortable, and marched back over to his campsite. Mom murmured something to Dad, and I saw her eyebrows raise as high as they could go. It was her classic *I'm irritated at you and you better fix it* look.

"Eve, do you want to get started on dinner with me? I think we decided tonight would be tacos," Amy called out, interrupting whatever hushed conversation my parents were having.

"Sure, Ames, I'll be over in a second," Mom replied. I swiftly turned my attention to Margot and Ella, who were standing next to me.

"You know what that means, right?" I said slyly.

The sisters looked at each other before focusing back on me. "It means," Ella drawled, "that we have time to go explore the Thicket."

•   •   •   •   •

My feet pounded against the forest floor, my arms pumping rhythmically as I ran. I ignored the sharp slices of pain as the dune grass cut into my calves and thighs, leaving small red welts in their wake. Strands of hair blurred my vision as they fell out of my long braid again. The Thicket spread out for miles around me, but the vastness of it only made me feel... calm. I let my feet slow as it appeared in my view. "Ah, here it is," I whispered, mostly to myself, as Ella and Margot trailed behind me.

The tree.

The first year Ella and Margot joined us for camping, we wandered around the Thicket for hours each day. During that time, we discovered a special tree that we adopted as our own. Its massive trunk split in two directions, with one of those two branches splitting further into a Y, creating a perfect sitting spot. The branches of the Y grew upward, providing several more ideal climbing fixtures. The other big branch forking off from the trunk extended at an awkward ninety-degree angle for a couple feet before straightening out into a nice upside-down "L" shape. It took years for me to master ascending the numerous slippery branches covered in slick moss.

What made this tree, *our* tree, unique, was that it presented exceptional "sitting" spots for all three of us girls. Ella usually sat in the Y and Margot planted herself on the flat part of the L branch. I took my spot a step farther (and higher, for that matter) than the sisters and found a place a couple feet above the Y intersection that Ella sat in. I enjoyed being so high up that I could see small birds flitting across the treetops, gathering debris for their nests or bringing worms to their babies. I appreciated the safety I felt, even at an elevated area, where I could breathe in the salty air and be alone with my thoughts. But it wasn't just our notable spots in the tree that made it ours. It was the conversations, the heart-to-hearts, that Ella, Margot, and I would share while we were sitting in that tree. Even though Margot was only eight years old, it didn't stop us from chatting away. We'd tell our darkest secrets and our most embarrassing moments. Laughter would fill the air right before our tears, and both could only be heard by the quiet forest around us. We would bare our souls while we perched in our designated spots, hoping the forest would hear our skeletons and keep our secrets, too.

Ella and Margot at last caught up to me, their breath hot in my ear as they nearly doubled over.

"Geez, Willow, you could've slowed down some." Ella cracked a smile even though she held her arm around her stomach firmly, trying desperately to catch her breath.

Margot snorted. "Willow never slows down for us, Ella. You should know this by now."

I shot her a grin before digging my toe into the bark of our special tree and grabbing above me for a branch to anchor my weight. A few minutes later, we all perched in our respective spots, and silence took over.

I gently touched the moss that was clinging to the tree bark, its green spongy surface feeling soft beneath my fingers. Thoughts raced through my head as I eyed the small slice of beautiful nature in front of me.

"My parents are in a weird funk right now," I spoke up suddenly, my voice sounding strange in my ears as I said the words aloud. I hadn't even allowed myself to process the disturbances that swallowed our home recently. It was nothing too serious, just more arguing, some drinking, and a few escalated fights between Mom and Dad.

"What do you mean? They seemed okay earlier," Ella said gently, glancing up at me from her branch.

"Mom figured out Dad was drinking. Like, really drinking. He actually went to rehab a few months ago," I said, staring at the rubber toe of my converse, trying to blink back the tears.

"Oh, Willow, I'm sorry. Is he doing better now?" Ella asked. I could see Margot out of the corner of my eye and knew she was listening intently but letting Ella guide the conversation. I wasn't sure Margot fully understood the depth and depravity of alcoholism or rehab, but she listened attentively anyway.

"Well, that's the thing. He's been sober for three months now. But it seems like ever since he came back from rehab, my parents' relationship has been…worse." My voice broke on the last word.

Ella reached up to me, her pale fingers extended. I smiled sadly before placing my hand in hers.

"We're here for you. You never know, maybe this trip will be good for them. Perhaps they'll bond more..." She said the last part while raising her eyebrows and smiling.

"Ew, Ella! I do *not* want to think about that!" I shouted, laughing as I ripped my hand from hers.

Margot covered her hand with her mouth and giggled. "Ella's right. Maybe having sex in a tent will bond them more and—"

"Stop! We are done with this whole conversation! And Margot, you're too young to even know that word!" I could barely get the words out through my laughter. "On another note," I continued, "we should get back soon. Ella and I have to take some senior photos tonight on the beach."

Margot nodded, carefully placing her feet below her as she scaled down from her mossy-covered spot. Ella was next, nearly slipping at the last second before regaining her balance and landing on the forest floor with a *thump*. I followed her, the climb down from my position easy, as I was accustomed to it. Once I landed and we were trudging single-file back to our campsite, I threw my head over my right shoulder at them.

"You know, you're going to regret it if the 'bonding' statement you made earlier comes true," I said mischievously.

"Why's that?" Margot asked.

"Because," I said with a smile, "we're all sleeping in tents right next to them."

•　•　•　•　•

The photo excursion on the beach occurred after dinner, only taking about an hour and going smoothly, even with the wind having a nasty bite to it. Mom was the photographer. It was her side gig, and she enjoyed capturing important moments. Ella sported a dusty pink, full-length romper, and I wore a long-sleeve blue sundress. We were just wrapping up and working our way back to the campsite when Coach veered off the beach path into the outskirts of the Thicket.

"Coach!" Mom and I yelled simultaneously. I dropped my sandals I was carrying onto the sandy path and slipped my feet into them.

"I'll grab him," I told the others, making my way through the dense undergrowth. My dark blue sundress flowed right above my knees, protecting my thighs from the stinging grass. I spotted Coach just a few feet ahead of me, his furry back the only visible part of him through the copious plants. He was rolling in something, pushing his head onto the ground and rubbing his nose in whatever it was. I finally reached him and immediately recoiled.

"Mom! He's rubbing in a dead bird!" I shouted, trying to stifle a laugh that was half-humor and half-disgust. Mom placed her hand on her forehead and sighed.

"I mean, I'm not really surprised," Ella called out to me.

I flipped a middle finger at her jokingly and glanced back at my dog, who was still wiping his head insistently on the deceased bird. Reaching for his red collar, I pulled the sleeve of my dress over my nose to block the pungent smell of death permeating the air.

"Coach," my voice came out muffled through my dress. "Coach, come on," I repeated, tugging on his dirty collar.

He eventually lifted his head, his brown eyes bright and his tongue lolling out of the side of his mouth. I crinkled my nose in disgust as he got up and let me tug him away from the seagull.

"You smell disgusting," I said, letting my sleeve drop from around my nose and mouth. Coach licked my leg, and I yelped, jumping back from him.

"Gross! I don't want your dead bird breath on my leg!" I yelled.

Fits of laughter erupted from Ella, Margot, and Mom, who were waiting by the path.

"It's not funny!" I shrieked, even as I sensed my own laughter bubbling in my throat.

"It's hilarious! And what's even funnier is that your mom snapped a photo of it!" Margot said, doubling over in laughter. I watched as Coach's black-and-white head bobbed in the dune grass, heading toward them.

"He's coming for you, now!" I declared loudly as I followed him through the forest.

Mom winced as she clipped Coach's leash back onto his collar. The sour smell permeating from Coach's head and neck had caused Ella and Margot to cover their noses. I could see both of their eyes watering as I caught up to them.

"We are definitely going to wash him at the spigot when we get back," Mom said as we trekked back toward our camp on the sandy path. I could feel the sand and dirt coating the bottoms of my feet through my sandals. I spied the spigot just a few campsites away from ours and sighed at the rickety old post and faucet handle coming out of the ground.

"I'll wash Coach's head off. I have to rinse my feet anyway," I muttered, grabbing the leash from Mom.

"We'll wait for you," Ella said, slowing her pace, Mom and Margot following suit. Mom shifted her camera bag to lift her camera out, clicking her way through the images she'd taken. I placed Coach under the faucet then turned it until the water was a steady stream onto his head. Coach had always been an easy-going dog. He would sit through any bath, walk off-leash if needed, and loved almost everyone. I say "almost" because I have always believed Coach has a danger radar. He can sense if a person has good intentions or not. If he decides they seem dangerous to him, he won't go near them. He's never bitten anyone, but I'm sure if we were in trouble, he would.

The cold rush of water against my hands as I scrubbed Coach's neck felt pleasant on my skin, which was still sticky from the ocean-kissed wind down at the beach. Coach gazed into my eyes, holding my stare intently.

"I love you, Coach," I whispered, giving his head one last rinse before dipping my feet under the faucet and letting him go.

"Ah, Coach!" I heard Margot squeal, followed by the sound of Coach shaking his wet fur.

"C'mon, Margot, you had to have seen that coming," I said, spinning the spigot handle until it turned off.

The four of us and Coach strolled back into our campsite, where a small fire was burning in the firepit. Dad and Larry were perched on either side of one picnic table, a cribbage board resting between them.

"I have fifteen-two, fifteen-four, and there ain't no more," I heard Dad say, frustration creasing his brows while he moved his peg forward four holes.

"Look who turned up! How were the photos?" Larry's eyes wrinkled in happiness as we approached.

"Good! We got some beautiful sunset photos of Ella and Willow to commemorate their senior year," Mom said warmly, looking down at the image displayed on the back of her camera.

"Oh, and Coach rolled on a dead bird," I butted in. Dad yanked his hand back from petting the fluffy dog.

"What?! And you let me pet him?" he nearly shrieked. Mom tilted her head back in laughter.

"We washed him off at the spigot before we got back. Relax, you big baby," she said affectionately, brushing a kiss against Dad's forehead. She turned her camera so he could see her photos, and he instantly smiled.

"That's a good one, Eve," he murmured.

"Are you showing the photos without me?" Amy's shrill voice cut through the campsite as she hurried over, her hair damp from one of the few showers at the campground. Amy rushed to Mom's side, peeking over her shoulder at the digital image.

"Amazing," she said breathlessly.

Curiosity overcame me, and I reluctantly ambled over, staring down at what everyone was fussing over. The photo was a full-body image of me, standing in the sand with my legs slightly crossed, the ocean on full display behind me. My left hand was placed on my right forearm, my blue sundress billowing around me. There was a soft, warm glow behind me from the sunset, and a small smile lit up my face. It *was* a beautiful image. I rested my head on Mom's shoulder, whispering, "Thank you," to her.

"Whatever you had for dinner tonight sure smelled great," a startling voice spoke out.

I whipped my head around, perturbed to find Christian at the border of his campsite and the Grisham's. Clad in a navy T-shirt and jeans, he shoved his hands into his pockets nonchalantly. No fire was sizzling at his campsite, which still remained fairly empty other than his blue tent and slightly beat-up car. He strode a little closer. "Smelled like tacos," he continued, lifting the edge of his lips into a smirk.

"Yeah, it was tacos. You've got a good nose," Amy said quickly.

"Wish I could cook like that. I was never taught how to cook. I'm mainly self-taught, but my skills clearly aren't up to par with yours," Christian went on.

Mom let out a nervous laugh.

"If you thought Amy's tacos smelled good, you should really try my wife's brownies. They are out of this world," Dad said, placing his cards down on the table and returning to his game with Larry.

"Oh, brownies? I love brownies," Christian said. The tone of his voice and his gaze shifting to me made my skin crawl, goosebumps appearing on my arms.

"Well, why don't you come try one? We were about to eat a few anyway," Dad inquired, nodding his head toward Mom. I detected Mom shooting Dad a quick glare, but he had already turned back as Larry counted his points for that round. After a few tense seconds, Mom swiftly turned on her heel toward the back of our Expedition, which sat with the trunk open. She dug around for a couple moments before pulling out a Tupperware with a purple lid.

"Yeah, Christian, why don't you sit down and try a brownie?" she eventually spoke up. She had clearly chosen to trust Dad's judgment.

My mouth nearly dropped open. I was appalled. My parents, who taught me never even to speak to a stranger, were inviting a completely random man camping next to us to just sit down and eat a brownie?

Unbelievable, I thought bitterly.

Then again, maybe not that unbelievable, since they believed me in the past, and I turned out to be wrong.

"Sure, I'd love to try one!" Christian said eagerly. He crossed through the Grisham's into our campsite and was about to sit down at the picnic table when an explosion of barking erupted. Ella instinctively grabbed my arm, her round green eyes shifting to mine.

"Coach, stop that!" Mom rushed by, slamming the brownie container onto the picnic table and seizing Coach's collar. "I'm so sorry about him, he's really out of sorts today," she commented, leading the dog away from the picnic table and chaining him to a nearby tree. His ears drooped momentarily, and I felt a pang of pity in my chest.

It's not his fault he and I both sense something off with Christian.

"All is forgiven since you offered me this delicious brownie. These are incredible!" Christian said, shoving a big bite of gooey chocolate dessert into his mouth.

I refrained from rolling my eyes. Mom was beaming. She always loved when people complimented her food. And rightfully so, because she was a talented cook. My eyes roamed suspiciously over our campsite. Christian sat comfortably with Dad and Larry at the table, his eyes assessing the cribbage board and cards laid out. All three had begun some small talk, and I could scarcely hear Dad bringing up what kind of weather we were supposed to have this weekend. Amy and Mom huddled near the matching camp kitchens, their heads leaning together and conversing quietly while scrubbing the dinner dishes. Coach still sat tied to the tree, whining and panting. Ella and Margot stood on either side of me, and Ella's grip on my arm had loosened a few seconds before. I realized how awkward we probably looked, just standing in the middle of the campsite while others were playing games or talking.

I opened my mouth, about to ask them if they wanted to take Coach for a walk, when Larry piped up from the table, "Hey girls, do you want to play crib? Christian here says he's played it before and wants to challenge ya."

I felt Margot tense next to me. A quick battle began inside my head—this man made me uncomfortable, and he obviously made Ella and Margot feel the same, but he wasn't going anywhere. Our parents trusted him, at least enough to let him sit at our table, eat our dessert, and play games with us. I took a step forward and lifted my chin, my eyes hardening.

"Sure. I'll play him first," I declared.

If there was one thing I felt confident I could do right then, it was beat this asshole in a game of cribbage.

CHAPTER 3

Shortly after the game began, it became crystal clear that Christian had not played cribbage before, despite what he told Larry. As soon as it was his turn to count up his points, he stumbled over his words and muttered something about not remembering the exact rules.

"So, you have fifteen-two because these two cards equal fifteen, then you have a pair of fours, so that's four points total," Margot explained in her sassy eight-year-old voice, reaching over to Christian's cards and pointing to them accordingly.

"Oh, right," Christian's words came out a little too loudly, as if he was trying to be convincing. I raised my eyebrows at him and gestured to the board.

"So, move your peg four holes," I said, my voice dripping with annoyance.

Christian's hand moved swiftly to his peg, placing it four holes ahead of where it had been. Normally, I would have been very polite, even quiet, with strangers. Christian's strange demeanor had gotten under my skin, so I was slipping easily into sarcasm and sass in defense. His piercing dark eyes lifted to mine, the swirling irises beady underneath his dark lashes. For a moment, I thought I detected a hint of playfulness in his steady gaze. He lifted the corner of lips lazily into a smirk and said, "Your turn."

Unsurprisingly, I won the game. I still wasn't Christian's biggest fan, but he gained a few points by telling me about his job at Amazon. He also explained how he moved to Washington state six months ago and currently resided in the city of Renton. Not enough detail to shake my caution off, but at least he could hold small talk and open up a little. I couldn't quite place the look he had given me earlier across the table. He had looked at me plenty during the game, but the penetrating stare given to me struck me as odd. It was...playful? Challenging? I wasn't sure.

Christian excused himself after the game was finished, wandering over to his camping chair and plopping down. I glanced away from him and up at the skies, admiring the thousands of twinkling stars spread above me. Inhaling the salty air through my nose, I continued to stare at the glittering, inky sky until I felt a hand on my back and turned to see Dad standing next to me.

"It always seems that more stars are visible here than at home," he whispered, his gaze fixed upward.

"It does," I said softly. Coach had been unchained from the tree as soon as Christian had returned to his campsite, and the soft, tricolor Australian Shepherd trotted over to us, prodding my hand with his nose.

"I think Coach is ready for bed," I told Dad.

"Well, you girls need to get to bed anyway. Beach day is tomorrow."

I nodded absentmindedly, stroking Coach's head and staring at the smattering of stars contrasting with the jet black sky. I was always at my most relaxed when I was outside in cool, fresh air.

"Come on, Willow! Let's brush our teeth," I heard Margot's voice and turned to see her and Ella standing side-by-side, toothbrushes in hand. I gave Dad a short hug and smile then walked to the tent I shared with my best friend. My hefty, black duffel bag sat inside, full to the brim. I was a consistent overpacker. When packing for trips, I would count one item of clothing for each day then double it. This trip, we'd be gone for four days, so I'd packed eight shirts, eight shorts, eight pairs of underwear, and so on. I also packed a whole outfit for flashlight tag, which happened on Saturday night.

I unzipped the bag and began digging through the contents, searching for my toiletry bag. I silently cursed myself for overpacking as I pushed through various clothing items. As my hand finally grasped the small purple carrier, I let out a yelp of triumph.

There you are.

"Willow, come ON!"

Despite my hearing loss, Margot stomping her feet in frustration outside the tent filled my ears. I left my duffel partially unzipped to replace the toiletry bag when I got back and exited our small tent. As soon as the brisk, chilly night brushed against my skin, I immediately turned back around.

"Hold up, I need a sweatshirt! It's freezing out here now!" I exclaimed.

Doubling back to the tent, I reached in my duffel and felt around until I found one of my most worn sweatshirts with an image of a tiger on the front. While I loved this sweatshirt, it wasn't my absolute favorite. Everyone knows not to take their most valued clothing items camping in case they get ruined or eternally smell like campfires—it's Camping 101.

I pulled the gray hoodie over my head, which caused my braid to become nearly undone. Reaching my hand up, I felt the top of my hair, groaning when I identified the frizz and knots beginning to form. Rushing over to where Ella and Margot were now waiting at the edge of the campsite, I noticed Margot with her arms crossed and an irritable look on her face.

"You took *forever*," she claimed, turning on her heel to walk toward the bathrooms.

Ella glanced at me and laughed as she held her arms up in defeat.

"I didn't know we were in a time crunch," I muttered under my breath.

I stole a quick glimpse at Christian's campsite, which appeared completely dark due to the absence of a campfire. I assumed he had gone to bed, but movement caught the edge of my vision, and I paused. Christian was still awake, sitting in his chair in the shadows, staring again at the empty fire pit. He had no phone in his hand, no book, nothing to occupy him except his own thoughts, I supposed. His brown hair was messy, his body limp as he simply gaped at the gray ashes left behind from previous fires in the pit.

"Willow?" Ella's voice broke through my unsettling thoughts.

"Sorry, let's keep going," I said, picking up my pace. After talking more with Christian earlier, I wanted to give him the benefit of the doubt. But how many people just sit with a blank stare at an empty fire pit in the pitch black of night?

The restrooms were located in one building with a few big individual stalls in the front and a couple in the back, along with three individual showers. People often tracked wet sand in, sometimes didn't flush, or left a stench so strong I would pull my shirt over my nose while I peed as fast as I could.

Under normal circumstances, I loved having privacy, but each year since the Grishams had joined us for this trip, Ella, Margot, and I had always shared an individual bathroom to brush our teeth at night. Safety in numbers. The bathrooms were in the center of the campground loop, a good minute walk from our campsite. Squinting through the dark night, I could narrowly make out our white EZ-Up awning from where I stood outside the stalls. Ella knocked on one of the doors, and when no one responded, swung it open. The single fluorescent bulb barely illuminated the bathroom. I heard Margot switch the lock on the door as I surveyed the bathroom, keeping my toiletry bag tucked under my arm. A toilet sat in the corner, a mirror to its left, accompanied by a sink with an air-dryer for hands mounted on the wall. An orb-weaver spider had spun its web in the upper corner above the mirror, its long, spindly legs spreading out onto its carefully crafted masterpiece.

"Gotta love these exquisite bathrooms," Ella said sarcastically, pushing toothpaste onto her toothbrush. I snorted, staring at the sand wedged between every crevice of the floor.

"The maintenance workers must not be on their game this year. I feel like last year it was much cleaner," I said.

I rustled around in my small bag until I found my toothbrush and toothpaste. Margot was brushing her own teeth and wandering around the bathroom, humming as she walked. The bathrooms were spacious, I'll give them that. Four or five people could easily fit in one before it started feeling crowded. We all spit out our toothpaste and took turns using the toilet before leaving the stall.

We were quiet as we walked back to our campsites, our path only lit by the small camping lantern Margot brought with her. I could now see that Larry and Dad were awake at the campfire, their faces aglow from the warm orange flames that danced around the pit.

When we were only a few feet from our tent, Margot piped up, "What do you think will happen this year?"

"What?" Ella and I asked simultaneously, confused by her question.

"Every year, something weird happens. Sometimes, it's something small, like Eve forgot the ground beef for tacos, and we had to eat hot dogs in tortilla shells instead. But other times, it's big, like that year those strange people stayed up all night wearing animal heads and chanting by the fire." Margot took a breath before continuing. "What do you think will happen this year? Will it be a big year, or a small year?" She tilted her head toward us.

A laugh rumbled in my throat. She was right. A couple years ago, a group of people in their mid-twenties camped across from us. They would sleep all day then wake up around 4 p.m., put on giant stuffed animal heads, and chant around the campfire. The creepiest part was they had a newborn baby with them. I remember Mom and Amy gawking at them and whispering to themselves about whether they should offer to take the baby. It seemed unhealthy for a newborn to be seemingly ignored throughout the day, and then be awake all night, let alone get passed roughly around a campfire while people sang and danced and drank.

"Man, that was a weird year," Ella said, chuckling as she unzipped the tent.

I caught a glimpse of shadowy movement in the corner of my eye. Christian was standing at his tent, his eyes fixed on Dad and Larry. He continued staring at them for a few seconds then shook his head slightly, as if shaking off his thoughts, before climbing into his tent. A feeling of uneasiness rose within me, but I shoved it down. Coach came trotting up to us, his eyes tired, and walked right into our tent. I watched from outside as he curled himself up into a ball near the end of my sleeping bag. Margot walked toward Larry and Amy's tent, where she'd be sleeping. As Ella and I clambered into our tent, I turned around and glanced at Margot, who was now stepping into the tent with her mom.

"Well," I muttered under my breath, "I really hope this will be a small year, but something tells me it might be a big one."

• • • • •

The tough undergrowth of the ground digging into my ribs awoke me the next morning. I rolled over and opened my eyes blearily, reaching to rub a knot that had formed in my lower back. Even with several blankets and my sleeping bag underneath me, I was able to feel the hard earth through the bottom of the tent. I groaned softly and yanked my sleeping bag over my head to block out the bright morning light filtering through the tent's flimsy material. Coach was keeping my feet warm, still fast asleep with his body curled up tightly. I knew without even looking that Ella wasn't in the tent. She was an early riser and usually got up before everyone else. Under the cocooned warmth of my sleeping bag, I tried to close my eyes and fall back into the deep, wonderful sleep I had been having, but soon the dazzling sunlight was too bright to ignore. My good ear scarcely distinguished the birds cawing, feet shuffling, and ocean waves crashing. I groaned again, pulling my phone out and checking the time. It was only 7:32 a.m. How was it so light at 7:32 a.m.?

I gently brushed my fingers across Coach's back and murmured his name to rouse him. He blinked at me sleepily and let out a big yawn.

"Oooh, big yawn," I said softly, scratching behind his ears as he got up and stretched.

I scooched to the edge of the tent and quietly unzipped it, slipping my tennis shoes on and letting Coach out. The bright morning light assaulted my vision, causing me to wince and briefly cover my eyes with my hands.

"Look who's awake," I heard Dad say. I rolled my eyes.

"It's way too early," I said, joining my parents, Larry, and Ella at the picnic table.

"Margot and Amy aren't awake yet?" I asked Ella.

"No, you know they can both sleep through anything. And they're grumpy as hell if you try to wake them," Ella said, stirring her hot chocolate. I nearly salivated just looking at it.

Mom hopped up from the table when she noticed my expression and poured some hot water from the kettle into my special mug. Rubbing my eyes, I plopped down at the picnic table. Mom placed the mug in front of me and handed me a hot chocolate packet and a spoon.

"Thank you," I murmured. Ripping the hot chocolate packet open, I dumped the contents into the warm cup, slowly stirring it. The sweet aroma filled my nostrils, and I grabbed the mug, placing it to my lips and sipping.

"What's for breakfast?" Ella asked Mom.

"Breakfast burritos," Mom stated simply, taking her place again at the table.

Thank God I thought to myself. Breakfast burritos were among my favorite breakfast foods. I took another sip of my hot chocolate, the scalding liquid leaving a rough feeling on my tongue. The cold and empty fire pit must have captured Larry's attention because he got up from the table and began stacking wood inside it.

A few minutes later, Amy stumbled out of her tent as Mom started making the burritos, and Margot emerged soon after. Expectedly, they were both groggy and grumpy as they sat in front of the warm fire with their own mugs of hot cocoa. Soon, the breakfast burritos were ready to be assembled, and we each filed into a line in front of the grill. I loaded a soft tortilla with eggs, cheese, and sausage. Once we were all seated with our breakfast burritos, silence ensued, leaving only the sound of quiet chewing filling the air.

"When are we heading down to the beach for beach day?" Margot asked, breaking into the comfortable quiet.

"Probably around eleven or so. Don't forget to bring a book or a volleyball or something to do while at the beach," Larry answered before taking another big bite of his burrito, sausage falling onto his plate.

We had dubbed Friday as "beach day" each year, which consisted of us walking the short route to the beautiful dunes and rushing water. We usually spent a couple hours reading on beach towels, flying kites, or passing a volleyball back and forth. How long we spent there often depended on the weather. Westport was known for being a chilly city sprinkled with sporadic sunny days. There had been several years where beach day ended early due to dark clouds coming in, followed by rainfall.

I peered out from the cover of the awning to observe the sky. It was blue and clear with a few clouds drifting around aimlessly. I was about to pipe up about how the weather seemed to be perfect for a day on the beach when Coach perked his ears up, staring at Christian's campsite. I followed his gaze and spied Christian unzipping his tent, stumbling onto the ground like he was intoxicated. He regained his balance and stood up, brushing the dirt off himself.

"You okay over there?" Dad's voice boomed out.

"Oh, yeah, I'm fine! Just not a morning person!" Christian held up a hand in greeting before sinking down in his camp chair. Dad shrugged, focusing on his burrito again.

"Do you have a beach day, too?" Margot yelled over at Christian. I smacked my hand against my forehead. Sometimes I forgot Margot was still young, which often meant she had no filter and was way too trusting of people.

Christian pushed himself out of his chair and crossed into our campsite comfortably, eyeing Margot. I frowned, setting my burrito down as I wondered what he was going to say.

"Beach day? Hmm, I can't say I've ever done a full beach day. I've had my fair share of lonely beach walks, but never a whole day dedicated to the beach," Christian said, his gaze never leaving Margot. Amy shifted in her seat, and I caught a quick glance exchanged between her and Larry.

"You could join our beach day," Margot continued, shoving a bite of burrito in her mouth. I sighed and shook my head.

"Honey, that is really nice of you but–," Amy started to say.

"Actually," Christian cut Amy off, his dark eyes glinting in the morning sun, "a day full of fun on the beach with you guys sounds awesome." Before anyone could interject, he turned on his heel and plodded back over to his tent, zipping it behind him.

"Are you guys seriously letting this stranger join us for beach day?" I bit out, slamming my mug down on the table.

After some short whispers between her and her husband, Amy shrugged her shoulders. "It's a free country. We can't stop him from coming to the beach."

My head swung dramatically to Mom, who stood with her coffee mug in her hand at the camp stove. Surely, she would not let this strange man join us for what was supposed to be a happy day at the beach? Mom was one of the most protective parents I had encountered. Even though Christian hadn't truly done anything to make anyone uncomfortable, didn't she feel...*off* about him? I nearly recoiled as Mom shrugged her shoulders, just as Amy had.

"It is what it is, Willow. You don't have to interact with him if you don't want to. But don't be rude, okay? He seems like a nice guy. He's probably just a little lonely."

Ella groaned from across the table. "I know we're trying to be inclusive, and I have nothing against the guy. It just seems a little weird that we're inviting him to be part of *our* tradition," she said as she twirled her hot chocolate spoon around in her mug.

Finally, someone that agrees with me.

"Like Eve said, El, don't be rude to him," Margot voiced. She sprung up from the table and quickly announced she was going to get ready and was excited we had a new "friend" joining us. Shaking my head, I gazed at Ella, who was rolling her eyes at her little sister.

Christian exited his tent quietly, clad in swim trunks and a zip-up hoodie. He wore sunglasses and a smug expression and had a beach towel tucked under one arm. I glanced at my phone, which read only 9:36 a.m.

"You're a little early." I couldn't help the snide comment slipping from my lips so easily. The irritation was bubbling under my skin, clawing for a way out.

Christian ruffled his short brown hair, a grin tugging at his lips. "I actually was going to go claim a spot for us. It's a nice day. The beach is bound to be busy. You folks take your time, and I'll go set up." His words flowed smoothly as he removed his sunglasses and stared at me, a silent dare for me to comment back. I chewed the inside of my lip, trying forcibly to swallow the words I so badly wanted to say.

"That's kind of you, Christian. Thank you. We're going to get ready in a few, and we'll meet you down there," Mom said. Her smile reached her eyes and she looked genuinely...happy. Calm. I felt like I had been dropped into an alternate universe. My mother was usually not this undisturbed about strangers poking around in our business.

When I was thirteen, Mom and I had been shopping at a bookstore in Seattle when a homeless man began following me through the aisles. I was so engrossed in all the books that I didn't notice my surroundings. Being hard-of-hearing means you tend to tune out some smaller noises when you become focused on something. When Mom found me and saw the homeless man trailing behind me, she took her high heel off her own foot and threatened him with it.

Yes, my mother took off her own high heel and shoved it into a homeless man's face to get him to leave me alone.

He probably just wanted food or money.

That story was an accurate representation of Mom and her fierce protectiveness. It was so out of character for her to be so casual around someone we didn't know well. Same went for Dad *and* the Grishams. For all the time I had known them, Larry had always carried a pistol on him somewhere. Did that scream, "Let's invite a stranger into our campsite and feed him dinner and go to the beach with him"?

I didn't think so.

However, after a separate incident that occurred in Westport a few years ago, I wasn't sure my parents would ever believe me about anything again. I had lost their trust, and now when I was worried about something, they thought I was just being "dramatic."

I dropped my now-empty breakfast plate into the dirty dish bucket, along with my hot chocolate mug. Without saying a word to anyone, I called Coach over and ducked inside Ella's and my tent. The air inside was almost humid, despite it being a comfortable fifty-five outside. I didn't mind the warmth though, and I quickly nestled into my sleeping bag again with Coach at my side. Before I could close my eyes, the zipper to the tent screeched, and Ella poked her head in.

"Are you getting ready?"

I scoffed. "Does it look like I'm getting ready?"

"You don't have to take out your anger on me, Willow. I'm on your side."

I sighed. Ella kept going. "This is our last camping trip before we graduate high school. What if we're too busy with college stuff next summer to come here? We need to enjoy this. Every moment of it. It's our last huzzah."

"Did you just use the word 'huzzah'?" I snorted. After a few moments of silence, I took a deep breath and turned to face her. Her emerald eyes were full of concern.

"You're right. I'm sorry. I've been a bitch because Christian makes me uncomfortable. I shouldn't let it bother me the whole trip," I reached my hand out to touch hers, my official way of letting her know I heard her. That I truly was sorry.

She grinned and gripped my hand tighter, nearly rolling me over as she pulled. "Okay, now that that's over with, we both need to get ready. And we need to do it while *not* worrying or thinking about Christian." She laughed, stepping into the tent to join me.

Coach leapt up and licked her face, eager to greet her.

"Let's get ready then," I said as I pushed myself up into a sitting position. "Besides, what's the worst he can do when there are seven of us and only one of him?"

CHAPTER 4

About thirty minutes later, the seven of us were on our way to the beach. My flip-flops dug into the steep hill as we walked, flinging sand every time I took a step. My bag was heavy on my arm, filled with books, my volleyball, and snacks. I shielded my eyes from the sun with my hand as we reached the top of the hill that overlooked the beach.

Breathtaking.

Every year, I forgot how stunning the beach was. It wasn't a typical beach that most people think of, with picturesque white sandy shores and crystal-clear turquoise water rolling in on soft waves.

No, *this* was a Pacific Northwest beach.

The sand was a tough mixture of blacks, browns, and tans, gritty between my toes instead of soft and pillowy. The ocean somehow appeared both inviting and unforgiving, its relentless, dark, cold waves crashing to the shore with promises to take me underneath the surface. Adults and children alike sometimes dared to swim in the icy water, but only allowed themselves to wade a few feet in. Waist high. No one wanted to get caught in whatever lurked beneath the intimidating, deep blue waves. Despite what may have sounded like harsh conditions, as I stood and admired the scene before me, it brought immense peace to me, refilling my lungs with fresh salty air. The pebbly sand stretched out along the coast for miles, and it was the only thing separating the Pacific Ocean from the dune grass and forested area behind us.

A few groups of people strolled the beach. One group had driven their Ford F-150 nearly up to the water, assembling a fortress of umbrellas and beach towels around it for shade. A few feet ahead, two blonde-haired children sat happily in the grainy sand, building sand castles.

"Look, there's Christian, waiting for us!" Margot's shrill voice called out as she pointed to a big piece of driftwood over to our left.

Sure enough, Christian stood by the driftwood with a hand on his hip, the other hand lazily waving to us. I bit my lip, annoyance bubbling up inside me again. We had to share our tradition of beach day with a weird man who didn't even know us. Mom exchanged a quick glance with Dad, who responded with a brief approving nod toward Christian.

"Here we go," I muttered to Ella as we walked down the sandy beach.

After a few moments, the sand felt wet and gravelly between my sandal and the bottom of my foot. I jerked my flip-flops off one at a time, allowing my feet to sink into the ground with relief. Margot was already greeting Christian and setting her bag down by the driftwood.

"Remind me why kids are so trusting again?" I whispered to Ella. The sun was beaming from between the clouds and I quickly felt sweat bead on my neck underneath my gray hoodie.

"They don't know any better. They want to think everyone is a good person," she murmured back.

"There you guys are! Thought you'd never make it. Is this spot okay? I've never had an official 'beach day,' so I wasn't sure what the terms and conditions were." Christian's wink sent chills down my spine, despite the warmth of the sun still sizzling onto my skin.

"This is great, Christian. Thank you," Mom said smoothly.

Amy plopped her bag down next to Margot's and laid her towel out neatly. Mom followed suit, her red beach towel in stark contrast to Amy and Margot's green ones. Coach wandered over and sprawled out on Mom's towel at her feet, already attempting to sunbathe. He kept one eye open toward Christian at all times.

Larry and Dad began unpacking their prized possessions they brought each year for beach day— their kites.

Every year, they competed for whose kite could fly the longest, highest, fastest. It was a silly competition that lasted the whole time we stayed at the beach and usually included a lot of petty arguments between them and a lot of laughter between everyone else.

"Look, Willow, those people are setting up a volleyball net!" Ella's comment directed my attention away from the kite competition down the beach to where a group of people were setting up a net and perimeter in the sand.

"Will you play with me this year?" I turned to Ella, silently begging her with my best puppy-dog eyes to join me in my favorite sport.

"You know I suck at volleyball. If I asked you to play soccer with me, would you?" A smug grin tugged on Ella's lips.

"How about this? You play volleyball with me today, and if there is *ever* a soccer competition on this beach, you can count me in." My words came out in a rush.

Out of the corner of my eye, I could see the net was nearly ready to go. I wanted to ask them if I could join before the game started. Ella sighed and put her hand over her face before nodding her head. "Fine. But you owe me big time for this."

Ella and I tugged off our sweatshirts and placed our sandals near our moms, urging them to watch our stuff while we went to join the volleyball game.

"Have fun, sweetie." Mom's eyes twinkled as she squeezed my leg. My parents absolutely loved watching me play volleyball. It had been my main sport since I was in fifth grade, and I had worked hard to become the best I could be.

The cloudy sky had parted nicely since we had arrived, allowing the sun to blaze down steadily on us. It was only about seventy degrees, but it was enough to warm me. The ocean waves crashed harshly against the shore, wind whipping the water in different directions. As Ella and I sauntered up to the perimeter of the makeshift beach court, I took a headcount of the people already here. There were five people milling around, three of which were women in their twenties and two men who looked to be late twenties or early thirties. I waved my hand in greeting as we approached.

"Need any extra players?"

One of the guys with sandy blonde hair pumped his fist in the air.

"Yes, we need more! Thank goodness. Except, we really need three more people, and there's only two of you. We can't have an uneven number. Is there anyone else you know who'd be willing to play?"

The thought of Dad playing with us briefly crossed my mind. He was athletic and had been my coach in the past. The idea evaporated as quickly as it had come as I glanced upward and saw two kites sailing the skies, each trying to outdo the other.

Maybe I could rope Mom into playing?

"You guys look like you're trying to find another player!"

I sucked in a breath and shut my eyes.

No.

Christian jogged toward us, his sunglasses hiding his eyes, and his shorts and T-shirt revealing his pale skin.

Like a vampire, I thought to myself and chuckled.

The thought of staking him through the heart with a piece of wood sounded quite appealing.

"Dude, yes! We're going to play with teams of four..." the sandy-haired man said. He introduced himself as Noah and kept explaining the layout of the game and teams to Christian, but my gaze was focused on the net. I didn't know what game of his own Christian was playing, but clearly, he wasn't going to stop butting into our trip anytime soon. I closed my eyes and breathed in through my nose, out through my mouth. I needed to lock into my volleyball game headspace.

"You okay?" One of the women laid a hand on my shoulder, staring at me with concerned eyes. She had tanned skin and dark brown freckles dotting her nose and cheeks, her chestnut brown hair blowing gently in the wind. A volleyball was tucked under her other arm. I nodded at her.

"I'm fine, thanks. I'm Willow, by the way." I stuck my hand out.

The woman grasped my hand and shook. "I'm Brielle. What position do you normally play? I think you're on a team with me, Noah, and your friend,

Ella." Brielle gave me an encouraging smile that already made me feel better.

She leaned in and whispered, "I got the vibe you and that guy, Christian, don't really get along. So, I figured I'd put you on separate teams in case, you know, you wanted to get some anger out on him or something." Her smile had a mischievous glint to it now, making her chocolate eyes sparkle.

"I'm a setter. And you're right," I popped the ball out from under Brielle's arm before continuing, "I don't like him. And he's about to learn how deep that dislike runs."

•   •   •   •   •

As I took my place in front of the net, Christian stood impatiently on the opposite side. He was dragging his feet through the sand and stretching his arms.

He looked like he had never been on a volleyball court before, beach court or regular.

Ella was positioned behind me, with Noah next to her and Brielle by me. I learned as we got into our positions that Christian's female teammates were Alessia and Nykole. The other guy playing with them was Mike. Christian stuck out like a sore thumb amongst them, pale and dark-haired against their tall, blonde heads and tanned bodies. I caught a glimpse of Ella, who looked nervous. I definitely owed her one for joining me today.

"Balls up!" With that, Noah served the ball over the net, and the game began.

The first half of the volleyball game was calm, with both teams scoring points, laughing, and playing contently. Once the set was at 17-15, with my team in the lead, things heated up. I wanted to win, and we were only eight points from rejoicing in victory. I stepped up to the temporary perimeter to serve.

When I began playing volleyball in fifth grade, I quickly grew a deep love for the sport, playing it both in school and in the off-season at a separate gym. When I was fifteen, during an important game for my club team, I had been nervous to serve the ball on game point. It could make or break the entire game. As I had spun the ball nervously in my hand before serving, a previous statement from Mom had popped into my head. She told me at one point, "When you serve the ball, it's like you have ice in your veins. You're in the zone, and nothing can snap you out of it."

As I stood at the perimeter now, even though it wasn't game point, my mother's words echoed in my head once more. Christian stood across the court, squatting slightly as he waited for the ball to come over the net.

Ice in my veins.

I looked straight at Christian and raised the ball in the air. It contacted my hand and floated toward him. He pathetically attempted to dive into the sand and pass the ball, but he missed, earning us a point. I smirked. Ella turned around from the front row and gave me a thumbs up.

"Again," she mouthed to me silently. The score was 18-15 now.

Christian brushed off the sand that infiltrated the front of his clothing.

"Nice serve," he said.

Brielle tossed the ball to me as I prepared to serve again. This time, I was aiming for the front row, between where Mike and Nykole stood. Short serves usually catch players off-guard, since they're so uncommon. I took a deep breath and smacked the ball, eyeballing it as it dropped perfectly to the ground in the center of the front row.

"Geez, who taught you to serve like that?" Alessia hollered. Her tone was humorous, but I caught the whispering between Mike and Nykole as they hashed out a plan to be more prepared for my next serve.

The next ball I served was received by Alessia and hit over the net by Mike, who had a powerful arm. Even though I was ready and dove for the ball, my pass went out of bounds. The score was 19-16, with our team still in the lead.

Dammit.

Ella gave me a pat on the back. "Get the next one."

I dipped my chin at her, wiping the sandy debris off my palms. It was Mike's turn to serve. He had a solid topspin serve and had aced us a few times already. We needed to be ready. I bent my knees and placed my hands palm-up in the air, shifting my weight moderately to my toes to be prepared to dive if needed. Mike's serve came over the net quickly, and Brielle passed it to me. I set the ball to Noah, who wound up and hit the ball over, where it spun toward Christian. He made a measly attempt to stick out his foot and have the ball bounce off it, but was unsuccessful.

"Dude, we told you already, there's no kicking in volleyball!" Mike's irritated voice was like music to my ears. I wanted Christian to be embarrassed, as sad as that sounded.

The score was 20-16, with us leading. Ella stepped up to serve, and I grimaced as she performed an easy underhand serve across the court. Luckily, it went over the net. Not all of her serves did.

Nykole tried to trick us by sending the ball back over on the first pass, but Noah caught on and passed the ball over to Brielle, who pushed it to the other team's far corner and earned us another point.

Soon, the score was 24-19. We huddled up, sweat dripping off us as we gripped each other.

"Okay, one more point and we win. Let's just breathe and get the ball over the net. Nothing fancy." Brielle's words were muttered between gasps for air.

"Get me the ball. I know what to do," I stated firmly.

Noah shot me a glance. "Really? And what makes you so confident in that?"

I smiled at the group before nodding to Brielle. "Let's just say I have some anger to get out."

We let out a cheer after the huddle and broke off into our positions.

"One second, guys!" I called out. Jogging over to where Christian was standing on the other end of the court, I approached him and stuck my hand out.

"I want to make you a deal."

His eyebrows shot up as his eyes flitted down to my extended hand and back up to me. "A deal about what?"

"If we win the game on this next point, you leave my family alone. You don't talk to us, you don't butt into anything. You don't even *look* at us." I held his gaze steadily.

"And what if you don't win on this next point? What do I get then?" Christian pulled his lips into the lazy smirk that he loved so much. Chills ran down my spine, my gut clenching uncomfortably.

"You can eat dinner with us again tonight," I stated firmly. It was the most I was willing to bargain for. For a short moment, I thought Christian was going to tell me it wasn't a fair trade. His dark eyes briefly skipped over my body in a look that made me want to crawl inside a hole and never come out. My hand began to tremble. I prayed he didn't notice.

At last, Christian's clammy hand grabbed mine.

"You have a deal."

I ripped my hand away quickly and trotted back to my team's side of the court, where I placed myself in the front right side. The setter's spot. Ella clasped my arm, and I could feel the concern coming off her in waves as large as the ones rolling out in the ocean. "What the hell was that?"

"Don't worry about it."

My best friend gave me an exasperated look before taking her spot in the sand. I tapped Brielle's shoulder before she could serve.

"When the ball comes back over," I whispered, "pass it to me. But pass it tight to the net." She chewed on her lower lip, questioning my words.

"Tight to the net? What if they just spike it back down at us?" She tilted her head at me curiously.

"Just trust me," I said.

Brielle nodded hesitantly and backed away to the perimeter, where she hit a beautiful float serve to the other team. Mike passed the ball to Christian, who bumped it over to Alessia. Alessia set it back over to us.

This was it.

The ball came soaring over the net in an arc. Brielle passed it to me tight against the net, just as I had asked. I held both hands in the air, making it look as if I was going to set the ball for Noah to hit over. My eyes darted over to the other team and the empty hole in the middle of the court.

The Puka.

There's a brief moment before the setter contacts with the ball in which they are surveying the other team and looking for open holes. Sometimes, the open spot is in the middle of the court, which a coach once told me was dubbed "the Puka." It seems like it would be an easy place for someone to get the ball though, right? Wrong. Because it's in the middle of the court, usually players think their teammate is going to get it and vice versa. And because everyone thinks the *other* person is going to get the ball since it's such an easy spot... *no one* usually gets it. Kind of like a "bystander effect."

Think of the setter in volleyball like the quarterback in football. Most of the time, the quarterback is scrutinizing their own players and trying to give the ball to the open teammate.

Sometimes, they observe the other team and realize there's an open path for them to take themselves.

In that quick moment before I contacted the volleyball, I saw the Puka was wide open. At the last second, I flicked my left wrist and tipped the ball over the net straight into that gap.

Ice in my veins.

No one was prepared. The ball dropped on the other side. And we won.

Ella and Brielle's cheers erupted around me as Noah came over and patted me on the back.

"What a tip that was! I don't think any of us saw that coming! You setters must have a sixth sense or something." Brielle applauded me, her smile filling me with pride. I was only seventeen and playing with people older and more experienced than I was.

Mike, Alessia, Nykole, and Christian all lined up to shake our hands and give us the obligatory "good game" comments. I grinned at each one of them, stopping at Christian and letting his warm, sweaty hand grip mine. I forced myself to look into his sickening gaze and grasped his hand harder, my words coming out with a bite to them.

"Stay away from my family."

I released him before anyone would notice the odd exchange between us. Coach galloped over, licking my face repeatedly. My one good ear picked up distant yells of excitement, causing me to raise my hand over my eyes to block the sunlight. My parents, Larry, Amy, and Margot all fist-pumped the air. They had clearly been watching from their beach towels.

Ella and I thanked the strangers who had quickly become teammates to us before heading toward our families.

"I think I changed my mind. Volleyball is fun." Ella's comment made me throw my head back and laugh.

"I'm going to hold you to that next year," I told her.

We approached the set-up our parents and Margot had created while we played. Beach towels and umbrellas lay haphazardly across the sand, along with books, water bottles, and two kites.

Amy squealed in delight. "That was so fun to watch! I mean, we only caught the last few points, but what an exciting game, you two!"

Mom tousled my hair and pulled me in for a hug. "Hey, where did Christian run off to?"

Her question made me whip around, taking in the court that was now being disassembled by Brielle and Nykole. Christian was nowhere to be seen.

I turned back around and tried to seem nonchalant, shrugging my shoulders.

"Maybe he found something better to do."

CHAPTER 5

After showering and settling in for dinner that night, I didn't see Christian in his campsite. I hoped he had taken our deal to heart and would leave us alone. I stared down at the chili in my bowl, another famous camping meal Amy and Mom made annually.

"Margot, eat your chili please." Amy pointed to her youngest daughter's bowl, lifting her eyebrows. I gulped as the eight-year-old rolled her eyes in response to her mother's instruction. Larry paused with his spoon halfway in his mouth, his jaw open in shock. Amy and Larry were exceedingly strict about the girls showing them respect.

"Come with me, Margot." Amy abruptly stood up from the table. Ella shot me a troubled look as the two walked away from the rest of us, barely being out of earshot. Amy's annoyed voice was loud enough for the rest of the campground to hear. Dad cleared his throat.

"What colleges are you going to apply to, Ella?"

Ella grinned and set down her spoon. "I think I'll apply to Washington State University, and possibly the University of Idaho," she said proudly.

I forced a smile. As much as I missed spending time with her, my family was a Husky family through-and-through. I would be applying to the University of Washington.

"Willow, do you think you'll apply to any out-of-state colleges?" Larry asked.

I opened my mouth to respond, but movement caught the corner of my eye. Christian sauntered up to his campsite from the Thicket, his hood up and hands in his pockets. I eyed him as he jumped into his car and drove off quickly.

"Willow? Did you hear me?"

I jerked my head back toward Larry, realizing everyone left at the table was staring at me.

"Sorry, um, I may apply to the University of Montana since they have a strong biology program. Other than that, I think I'll stick to in-state colleges." I set down my spoon and leaned my head with my good ear toward the sound of Margot and Amy arguing. They were behind the Grisham's vehicle, but I couldn't make out anything they were saying.

"I can't believe you and Ella are already thinking about college! I remember when Amy and I sat through Lamaze class together when we were pregnant with you guys." Mom's eyes watered as she reached out and grasped my hand for a few seconds.

"Don't go all soft on her now, Eve." Dad chuckled.

Mom shook her head softly, her shiny brown hair hanging down in loose waves over her shoulders. "Come on," she said to Ella and me, "help me with the dinner dishes."

I was given the washing bin, where I scrubbed every dish then passed it to Ella, who had the rinsing bin. After Ella rinsed the dishes, they got passed to Margot, who had just returned from her conversation with her mother and was understandably shaken up. Rolling eyes in the Grisham family was something they didn't take lightly. It was clear Margot had been reprimanded and was upset about it. I felt bad for the young girl. She picked up a lot of her sassy behaviors from Ella.

As we went through the routine of cleaning the dishes, darkness fell upon us. The stars lit up the sky, but we still turned on various camping lanterns around the site. I scrubbed a crusty spot on the last pan, angling it toward the glow of the nearest camping lantern to ensure I cleaned it properly.

Headlights loomed behind me briefly, illuminating the pan just enough for me to tell I had missed a spot.

"Thank you to whoever just drove behind me," I muttered. Ella laughed, her hands still wrist-deep in the rinsing bucket.

"You'll be sorry when you see who you're thanking," she said, giggling.

I slipped the pan into the rinse bucket and turned around right as Christian exited his car.

"Oh, joy," I said in a monotone voice.

Margot beamed at me, her first sign of happiness since she got back from being scolded. "It's your favorite person!" she chimed in sarcastically.

"I am going to dump this bucket of gross dish water on you if you don't stop talking!" I joked as I picked the plastic tub up and pretended to pour it on her. Margot shrieked, throwing her drying towel onto my head and covering my eyes.

I swiftly set down the tub and yanked the towel off. Ella grabbed Margot with her wet hands and was twirling her around as Margot hollered through her laughter.

"Stop! Stop! I can't breathe!" the eight-year-old protested, eventually escaping her sister's grip and dropping onto the picnic table. We all took a moment and gasped for breath, the giggles finally ceasing.

"Girls, can you please rinse those tubs out and put them away? It's about time we all head to bed," Amy said, poking her head out from inside their red tent. We had eaten a late dinner, and my phone read 10 p.m.

We assured her we would. Grabbing each of our buckets, Margot, Ella, and I began the short trek to the spigot a few campsites down. Coach followed behind us, sniffing every available rock and bush. Approaching the faucet, Ella fumbled with her phone so she could turn its flashlight on.

"Let's wait here. Someone is using it right now," I said.

A man had his back turned toward us, brushing his teeth while water splashed around his feet. Ella finally got her flashlight on right as the man finished brushing. I watched as he rinsed his toothbrush off, shook it a few times, then turned toward us.

The beam radiating from Ella's phone shone directly onto the man.

Christian.

Coach leaned silently against the back of my legs. His faint growl was too quiet for me to hear, but I could feel the vibration of his throat against my calf. My heart skipped in my chest. The water sloshed around in the dish bucket as I strode defiantly past Christian and toward the spigot, Ella and Margot close behind. I didn't even have a free hand to defend myself if needed. I placed my bucket on the cement square below the faucet and turned around.

Christian grinned at us, his lips still wet.

"Goodnight, girls."

My pulse slowed as Christian stalked off toward his campsite.

"Where has he been? We haven't seen him since the beach," Margot inquired.

"I don't know. He's not really our friend, so we don't have to wonder about where he goes," Ella whispered gently. She bent down, handing her phone to Margot while she rinsed out the dish buckets.

"You don't have to be so mean when you talk about him. He's nice." Margot crossed her arms.

I sighed, not wanting an argument to ensue. Margot was still young, not fully understanding the weight of stranger danger. Once Ella was finished rinsing, we headed back to our campsite. Christian appeared to be in his tent. I didn't see the strange man anywhere in his campsite, and his car was where he had parked it earlier.

Sleepy goodnights were exchanged, and Ella and I clambered into our sleeping bags, Coach nestled between us. Ella's breathing slowed in a matter of minutes, her rhythmic breaths telling me she had fallen into a deep sleep. Coach's eyes were closed, his body twitching as he dreamt. I rolled to my other side, facing the tent door. Although my best friend and dog slept peacefully next to me, and my parents lay in the tent next to us, a deep feeling of unease crept into my chest.

No matter how many times Margot said she liked him, or my parents told me to stop being dramatic, I couldn't shake it.

I couldn't shake the gut feeling.

I imagined other campers slumbering in their tents, surrounded by friends or family, kids or pets. I pictured the birds and the squirrels settling into their nests, protecting their babies and eggs. Although it was unlikely, I visualized myself being the only one in the entire campground lying with my eyes wide open, staring at the polyester ceiling of the tent. Somehow, in the recesses of my mind, a thought wiggled its way through—I would never be the only one awake in this campground. Because a predator lay in wait.

Cautiously creeping through the dark shadows, one foot in front of the other, a predator prepared to pounce on his prey. He strategically set up every encounter, every moment to gain trust of those around him, hoping desperately he could strike then blend back into the shadows before being caught.

Something told me Christian was lying with his eyes wide open, too.

CHAPTER 6

"Up and at' em"

I barely made out the shouts coming from outside the tent. A moment passed before it started again.

"Up and at' em, girls!"

I groaned and placed my pillow over my head. Ella was surprisingly fast asleep next to me, her honey brown head full of curls facing the other direction. Reaching over Coach, I shook her shoulder. She mumbled something incoherent before rolling over and saying, "What?"

"They're doing what they do every year," I said.

Ella slapped her hands over her ears and sighed as the booming sounds of our dads' voices filled the tent.

On the Saturday of every trip we had taken to Westport together, our fathers had shaken our tent and yelled for us to get up and get dressed. It was a tradition on Saturday mornings for us to make the five-minute drive into town to get donuts. Not just any donuts—Little Richard's donuts. Little Richard's was not only the sole donut shop for miles, but baked some of the best donuts I'd ever tasted. Getting woken up aggressively wasn't ideal, but our dads had a fun time doing it.

"What time is it?" Ella mumbled. I clicked on my phone.

"6:37 a.m.," I said.

"Can't they wait until at least seven?" she protested.

I guess even early risers have their limits.

Coach laid his head on my chest gently, and I found my eyes drifting closed again, precious sleep overcoming me...

"Wake up! Wake up! It's donut time!"

Margot burst into our tent, her eyes wild as she leapt over me and onto her sister.

"Get off!" Ella complained. She shoved Margot off to the side, allowing Coach to exit the tent through the open flap Margot had left.

"Good morning to you, too," I lifted the pillow off of my head.

"We're getting donuts!" Margot said in a sing-song voice. Even though Margot usually wasn't an early bird, the possibility of getting donuts changed everything for her.

Dad shook the tent, bellowing, "We're leaving in five minutes. Better get ready."

Margot scrambled out, leaving us grumpily getting dressed in her wake.

Once Ella and I had thrown on sweats and sweatshirts, the true camping look, completed with dirty tennis shoes, we emerged from the tent. I didn't see Amy or Mom, but Margot sat on Larry's lap in front of the fire, swinging her legs impatiently. Dad jogged over to us and tossed me the keys to the Expedition. Confused, I fiddled with them in my hands for a moment before asking, "I'm driving?"

"We thought this year would be a little different. You and Ella are going into town to get donuts." Dad gestured backward to Larry and Margot. "The rest of us are staying here and getting breakfast started."

I pursed my lips together, trying not to let my excitement show too much. We had never been able to go into town by ourselves before since we didn't have our licenses until this year.

"Can't I go with them? Please?" Margot whined. I could sense that Margot had asked her dad this before Ella and I even got out of our tent, but the answer had been no. Margot put on her best puppy-dog eyes face and leaned into her dad, pleading.

"How good of a driver is Willow, Nick?" Larry asked with a sigh.

"She passed her driver's test, both written and physical, with flying colors. Even the parallel parking test. I also make her put her phone in the glovebox while she drives." Dad's voice was edged with pride.

Larry shook his head, meeting the eyes of his youngest daughter.

"Fine, go. But you better stick with them the entire time."

Margot shrieked in happiness, throwing her arms around Larry in a bear hug. As the three of us plodded toward the car, Dad exclaimed, "Wait, one more thing!"

He shoved a piece of paper in my hand. "Both of your moms want coffee. Here's their order. Get something for yourself, too."

"Ooh–"

"*Not* for you, Margot. Get a hot chocolate or something," Dad said. He slipped me a fifty-dollar bill and kissed the side of my head. "Be safe."

•   •   •   •   •

I parked the Expedition right outside the quaint donut shop. A couple people milled around outside, but it was otherwise quiet. As we shut the doors to the car, I turned to face the ocean, which loomed just feet ahead of us. The fascinating thing about Westport is that it's surrounded by water on three sides, making it probable you could see the looming blue depths of the sea from almost anywhere within the city.

"I think it'd be cool to live in a beach town," Ella said. The salty mist coming off the waves created a dampness to the air as we stared at the water.

"Let's go in before the apple fritters are sold out. You know how fast they go," I finally said. We knew all too well not to let the seemingly vacant street fool us.

Little Richard's opened at 6 a.m., and most of the donuts were sold out by 8 a.m. I yanked open the heavy door.

"I love that sound!" Margot said, cheering.

"What sound?" I asked, looking around for a possible source.

"Oh, the door chime. Sorry, I didn't know you couldn't hear it." Margot appeared crestfallen.

I grasped the small girl's hand in mine. "It's okay. I don't hear a lot of things."

We stepped through the entryway, and the warm smell of donuts and baked goods filled my nostrils. Old tables lined the store's front windows, and the counter that stood before us was stuffed with different pastries. The fare was mostly donuts, but a few shelves had scones, muffins, and Danishes.

"It smells so good in here." Ella inhaled deeply.

Once we selected our dozen donuts, we piled back into the Expedition.

"Can we please stop at Granny Hazel's?" Margot pleaded.

Granny Hazel's was a staple for visitors to Westport. It sold the best saltwater taffy and snacks, along with clothing, toys, and other trinkets. Our families usually stopped there on the last day of every trip.

"We're stopping tomorrow, remember? It's usually Sunday when we walk around town, then eat at Bennett's Fish Shack," Ella said. Margot pouted in the backseat but didn't try to persuade us further.

"Can you map us to that one coffee drive-thru we went to last year?" I asked Ella.

Out of the corner of my eye, I saw her pull up her maps app. She quickly shook her head.

"I have no service. I'm sure we can find it, though. It was on the main road back to the campsite, by the gas station, remember?" she explained, chewing her thumbnail.

I had a horrible sense of direction, so I didn't remember exactly where she was talking about. Pulling out onto the main road, I glanced in the rearview mirror. Not a car in sight, but the beautiful ocean thundered behind us.

"If you keep driving straight, it will be on the left in about a minute." Ella pointed ahead to where I could barely see a small white shack in the middle of a vacant lot. A short time later, we were in the drive-thru line with one car ahead of us, and I sighed in relief.

"See, you would've found it on your own," Margot piped up from the backseat.

I snorted. "No, I don't think I would have. But thanks, Margot."

Dark gray clouds loomed against the silvery sky, ready to pour at any minute. The car in front of us drove off, and we were greeted at the window of Whitecap Espresso by a friendly teenager who wore braces and too much mascara.

"Hi, we have an order of five drinks." I listed off each drink, ending with Margot's hot cocoa. Our dads never ordered coffee but understood the desperate compulsion we girls had for caffeine.

I barely heard the high-pitched screech of the espresso machine as the barista busied herself preparing our drinks. Instead, I focused on a fat raindrop that landed on the windshield. Groaning, I pivoted to face Ella.

"It's raining," I grumbled.

"It's Washington, of course it's raining. Yet, we're still here ordering iced coffee." She laughed, attempting to scroll through social media while her phone buffered.

"Well, you and I are. Our moms always need their hot drinks. Did you know my mom drinks a hot latte even when it's eighty degrees out? It's ridiculous," I scoffed.

The barista handed me a drink tray, flashing a big customer-service smile. I tried to hand her the rest of the money leftover from the donut purchase, but she held her hand up.

"Oh, sorry, I thought you knew. Your friend paid for you," she said cheerily.

I scrunched my eyebrows in confusion and glanced at Ella, who wore the same look of skepticism that I did.

"I'm sorry, who are you talking about?" Even as the words left my mouth, it dawned on me what she was going to say.

"The guy in front of you, he paid for your drinks, told me to put them on his card. He said you guys were friends and camping next to each other. How nice of him, right? You ordered a lot," the barista rattled on.

It had been Christian's car in front of us. He drove such a generic car that I hadn't even noticed it was him. There was a short silence before I gathered myself enough to thank the barista and pull out onto the main road.

"That was nice of Christian," Margot whispered quietly.

I swallowed, trying not to let it get to me. How did Christian even know we were going to get coffee? How did he time it so he was in front of us? He swore to me he would stay away from us after the volleyball game, but now...

Now, I wasn't so sure.

Suddenly, I felt like the volleyball game had been a small victory, an insignificant triumph in a much bigger match I wasn't aware I was a part of until now. It was like being points away from a win in cribbage, only to figure out your opponent gets to count their hand first.

And it felt like Christian was holding all the right cards.

CHAPTER 7

Dad thought it was nice that Christian paid for our coffee. He assured me not to worry, that Christian had probably been getting himself a cup of joe when he noticed we were in the car behind him and wished to do a nice gesture.

Mom said the same thing. She had even gone over to Christian's campsite and thanked him personally and was astonished when I wouldn't go with her.

The whole morning after getting back from the donut and coffee run, I had remained quiet. I didn't want to keep voicing my opinions since I continuously got shut down. I had been wrong in the past anyway, so who's to say that wasn't the case this time, too?

Frustrated, I grabbed a water bottle and settled into the loveseat camping chair next to Ella. Everyone else gathered around the picnic tables, conversing while eating the last of their hot dogs from lunch. Ella swallowed her last bite and gulped down her root beer, her eyes trained on the flames in front of us.

"Do you want to head into the Thicket?" Ella asked as she licked some fallen ketchup off of her thumb.

I peeked at the forested area behind us before flashing her a grin. "Let's go."

Minutes later, we settled into our respective places on our tree. Margot stayed behind to try to beat her own high score in Mario Kart on her Nintendo DS. Ella squished herself into the intersection of two thick branches, resting her head against the spongy moss. Just slightly above her, I breathed in deeply, allowing the fresh, earthy air to fill my lungs and relax me. A petite starling flew overhead toward our campsite, its dark wings contrasting against the bright green landscape around us.

"Did you know starlings can mimic human speech?" I said, pointing to the small bird as it landed near Christian's car.

"No, I didn't. Do you still want to be a zookeeper someday? Because you know a lot of random animal facts," Ella said.

"Yeah, I do. I need to go to a school with a good biology program. My parents are arguing over the University of Washington or Seattle Pacific University being the best choice," I replied softly. I talked little about my parental issues to my friends back at home, not wanting anyone to see past the front I put on.

Ella was silent, seeming to contemplate her next words.

"How do you think your parents are getting along on this trip?" she finally asked. I noticed her picking at the bark on the tree branch. My parents' laughter filled my one good ear, causing me to peer through the trees and notice them playing a game of cribbage.

"They seem...fine. Better than usual. Maybe being away from home is helping somehow." I shrugged.

Ella and I bantered for the next hour about different problems at school and at home, allowing ourselves to dump information on each other with no judgment.

Just as we were about to descend from the tree we cherished so much, another starling flew by and landed on a nearby branch. It tilted its head at us, fluffing its wings out briefly.

"Say something and see if it copies you!" Ella said, nudging my foot.

I faced the starling, surprised it was still perching so close, and opened my mouth to say something silly. Before I could utter any words, the starling parted its beak and spoke.

"I see you."

Chills broke out over my forearms. Ella whipped her head around toward our campsite, eyeing it carefully through the trees.

"Maybe Margot said it as a joke and hoped it would repeat it back to us." Her voice was wobbly.

I followed her gaze toward our campsite. Mom, Amy, and Margot were napping in their camping chairs, Coach resting by Mom's feet. Larry and Dad were nowhere to be seen.

"I see you."

The bird's shrill mimic nearly made me lose my balance. I quickly scampered down the tree just as Ella did, needing to feel solid ground beneath my feet.

The bird bent its head down at us.

"I see you I see you I see you."

I jumped up and waved my arms in the air frantically, needing its sharp, trilling voice to go away.

"Shoo, you crazy bird!" I blurted out. The starling finally spread its wings and fluttered through the Thicket, eventually resting on the back of Christian's car. My stomach dropped as I saw the back of his blue camping chair, a hand outstretched from the person sitting in it. The starling reached out and pecked some sort of food from the person's palm before flying off. I didn't need to ask Ella if she was watching—I could feel her shaky breath on the back of my neck as we both continued gaping at what was unfolding before us.

Christian stood from his chair, shielding his eyes from the sunlight as he watched the starling soaring away. Ella gripped my wrist as our camping neighbor shifted himself to face the Thicket, to face us. I knew we were barely visible through the trees, but I still held my breath. Christian met our gaze as best he could and nodded once, confirming that yes, we should be scared.

That yes, he was always watching us.

CHAPTER 8

Ella and I never mentioned the starling's strange mimic to anyone. We decided that while it was highly suspicious that Christian fed the bird right after it spoke to us, no one would believe us, and we couldn't prove anything. Instead, we spent the rest of the afternoon taking turns playing Mario Kart on Margot's DS and challenging each other in Uno and Cribbage, although neither of us could focus on the games.

Around 8:30 p.m., Ella, Margot, and I slumped into our chairs, the fire aglow in front of us. The cracks of burning wood filled the air, and I shivered, tucking my hands into my sweatshirt sleeves. Larry and Dad sat at the table nearby, playing cribbage in the soft light of the camp lantern. Nestled in with a blanket wrapped tightly around her was Mom, reading a new thriller book she bought before our trip. My gaze shifted to Amy, who was braiding Margot's hair. Something flickered in my vision, and I turned my head, gripping the arms of my chair. A few seconds passed and then… I heard it. With my poor hearing, it was too difficult for me to make out the exact words, but I knew them anyway. A smile tugged at the corner of my mouth.

"Do you hear that?" I whispered to Ella, nodding my head toward the source of the sound. A couple seconds of silence occurred, followed by the yells and shouts we all knew well.

Margot's eyes lit up as the shouting echoed again. Her grin spread from ear to ear as she shouted, "Flashlight tag!"

Within minutes, the girls and I had stripped off our camping clothes and replaced them with all black garments. I wore black sweats over charcoal leggings to fight off the chilly air, along with a dark Hogwarts hoodie. My soot-colored Nike trainers were old and ratty, which was perfect for an event like flashlight tag. I placed my phone in Mom's delicate hands. If I took it with me, I would just wonder the whole time if it would fall out of my pocket and get lost. I noticed Ella pass her phone to Amy and grab a sturdy flashlight off the table. Dad strolled over to me, a dark object in his left hand.

"I bought this specifically for flashlight tag this year. It's powerful, so make sure you turn it off once you find a hiding place. It'll be great for when you're the 'counters,' though." He positioned the surprisingly lightweight item in my hand, and I glanced down at it.

It was smaller than I expected, smooth and able to fit in my pocket. I smiled up at him, grateful that he thought of things like this.

"Thanks, Dad. We'll be careful, I promise," I said to him, pocketing the flashlight into my sweatshirt.

"Flashlight tag! Flashlight tag! Meet at campsite 321 in *five* minutes for flashlight tag!" The group of kids, adults, and teenagers shouting in unison were passing our campsite, waving their flashlights in the air so the beams of light shot directly into the sky.

"You guys coming?" a familiar voice from the crowd startled me.

"Oh, Peyton! It's so good to see you!" I yelled back, recognizing the blonde, short-haired teenager among her siblings and family members.

Flashlight tag was an event that occurred every trip to Westport. Our family and the Grishams usually planned our annual trip for the second weekend of August, which also happened to be the weekend Peyton's family camped. I met Peyton in Westport at this very campground when we were both around nine. She had been biking with her siblings around the loop and asked if I wanted to join. Her toothy grin had been too hard to turn down.

Peyton had countless members of her family who also camped in Westport on the second week of August—cousins, aunts, uncles, second-cousins, and grandparents. One night every camping trip, Peyton and any willing family members pulled on dark clothing, grabbed flashlights, and walked around the loop, shouting to everybody that flashlight tag was happening. Each year, more and more families joined, eager to get their kids' energy out with a fun twist on hide-and-seek. By the time we usually started, the group tended to be mostly Peyton's family, with a sprinkle of spontaneous campers who were keen to attend.

"We'll see you at campsite 321 in just a couple minutes!" I yelled as Peyton's group drifted away, still shrieking out their invites to other campers. Peyton's blonde head bobbed as she nodded and gave me a thumbs up, roaming off with her family.

I turned back to Ella and Margot, who were double-checking that their flashlights had batteries.

"Margot, please wear your beanie. It's very brisk tonight," Amy said, handing her a navy cap. Margot sighed as she snatched the hat from her mother and grudgingly placed it on her head.

"There, happy now?" she retorted.

"Whoa, watch the attitude, or you won't be going at all," Larry called from the picnic table, where the game of cribbage between him and Dad had resumed.

"Sorry," Margot muttered, toying with the small flashlight she carried.

"Okay, we need to get going. We'll be back in an hour, an hour and a half tops," I said, giving Mom a side hug.

"You girls make sure to be safe. Go to Kyle if you need anything. We're going to come down there in two hours if you're not back," Dad said as he raised a hand in goodbye from the table. Kyle was Peyton's uncle who had led flashlight tag ever since I started going and probably before that.

Ella and Margot's eyes lit up with excitement. I felt the adrenaline winding up inside me, itching for a way out. I grabbed Margot's hand in mine.

"Let's go."

•   •   •   •   •

The path to flashlight tag was less-traveled, with only a handful of people knowing about it, let alone walking it. The common trails that led through the Thicket, up the sand dunes, and to the beach were marked officially by posts. This particular footpath didn't have a wooden post to identify it, but Kyle used it because it led to the perfect area for flashlight tag. There were easy landmarks that could be used as boundary markers and various hiding places to uncover. I stood quietly with Ella and Margot as last-minute campers joined our substantial group at the empty campsite 321, where the trail started.

"All right, everyone!" Kyle's voice boomed out among the crowd, which consisted of about sixty people. "Listen up! You're all going to follow me down the path to where flashlight tag takes place. Once we get there, please wait for my instructions before we begin. Those who are new, we're glad you joined. We hope you're prepared for playing on a chilly night. Now, let's move!"

The tall, athletic man gestured to follow him as he began trekking into the dark forest, his headlamp lighting the way. People started filing in behind him, like kids lining up for recess. The trail was only wide enough for two people to walk side-by-side, long grass and forest lining either side of the trail. We were heading straight into the Thicket, where I felt most comfortable, despite the looming darkness and dense trees. Margot turned her flashlight on as the people in front of us began trudging down the pathway. "Our turn," she whispered. Ella and I flicked our lights on as well, but I quickly switched mine off.

"I think we can see well enough with just your lights for now," I said to Ella and Margot, tucking my flashlight back into my pocket.

My breath came out in foggy puffs, and I pulled my hat down further over my ears. The walk to flashlight tag every year felt so momentous to me, not only due to the mysterious and dark forest surrounding us, but the energy of everyone. The only sounds I picked up on were muffled voices. My ears hardly detected the trees swaying in the wind. Adrenaline charged the air, filled with kids murmuring excitedly to their parents about where they wanted to hide and teenagers betting on how many people they'd tag out. The treetops spread above us, listening to every word and breath, every footstep we took. With the glow of several flashlights ahead of me, I could view the tops of a few people's heads, along with the thick trees on the outskirts of the path.

"Look, that'd be a good one to climb!" Margot murmured to me, pointing at a looming, mossy-covered tree a few feet ahead.

"Too bad it's not in the boundaries or else we could hide up there," Ella said, eyeing the massive branches that extended above us like thick spider legs.

"We're almost there," I noted, nodding my head toward the opening where the Thicket met the sand dunes. My heart was a steady pound in my chest, as if flashlight tag was a life-or-death event instead of a game. I guess the nervous system couldn't tell the difference.

After a few moments, Kyle was standing by the infamous, short wooden post sticking out of the sand. He waited patiently as everyone gathered around him at the base of the hill, leaning against the post with confidence. Once everyone settled, his voice boomed out again. Kyle was a firefighter, and his voice carried far and loud with an air of importance.

"Here's the rundown of the game for those who have never played. We'll split the group in half—half of you count and half of you hide. The point of the game is for the hiders to reach 'base,' which is this post, before a seeker finds you and shines their flashlight on you." He gestured to the wooden plank he leaned against before continuing. "*No* puppy-guarding the post. Counters, once you count down from 100 together, you spread out and look. You can tag people from afar if you see them and shine your light on them. After about ten minutes, I'll yell for everyone who is still hiding to come out, and we'll reset. Make sense?"

There were several fervent nods. One person called out, "So, if we hide the whole time and aren't found, but we don't try to reach base, do we technically still win?"

I rolled my eyes.

Amateurs.

"Where's your real skill if you don't weasel your way to base before someone finds you? That's the thrill of it," Kyle said, obviously unimpressed.

"I'll be at base the whole time, making sure things go smoothly. Now, let's talk boundaries," he went on, shining his flashlight to his left.

"That big, gnarly tree way over there is the boundary for the left side. That clump of smaller trees to my right is the boundary for the right side. The top of the hill," his flashlight beam shone on the top of the steep dune hill, the ocean out of sight on the other side, "is the other boundary. So, the playing ground is sort of a big triangle. And you can't go back down the path we came. It's off-limits," he said, shutting his flashlight off and turning his headlamp on. He whispered something in Peyton's ear, and she nodded before stepping forward.

"There are two ditches you should know about. People have twisted ankles, broken arms, and gotten hurt in other ways from these ditches. One of them is right here." Her words rang out quieter than her uncle's, but with the same touch of authority to them. The ditch she referred to was off to the left, a deep hole that was a couple feet wide. Dad had nearly fallen into it a couple years ago but luckily missed it by inches.

"The second ditch is closer to the top of the hill, toward the right. It's covered in dune grass, so it's harder to see. Be careful. Also, counters, turn your flashlights off when you're counting. Nobody likes cheaters." Peyton stepped back after shouting her final words.

I grinned and whispered to Ella, "One day, Peyton is going to take over for Kyle, you watch."

"I don't know if Kyle will ever give up his flashlight tag leader title. He likes to be in charge too much," Ella said, crossing her arms. Kyle divided us quickly into two groups of about thirty people each. Just as I hoped, Ella, Margot, and I were in the hiding group first. As soon as the seekers circled up and shouted out, counting down from 100, I grabbed the girls' wrists.

"I know where to hide," I said quietly, leading them into the fields of sharp grass. I flicked my light on and hiked down a worn path that was surrounded by brambles and bushes.

"Is it where we hid last year?" Margot asked from behind me. I bobbed my head quickly. There was a hedge ahead that we could crawl under and then into (yes, into), and be completely concealed from anyone's view. Ella, Margot, and I were the people crazy enough to have actually hollowed out the tiny branches from under the thorny hedge last year, making it easy for us to climb into once we got past the initial scratchy stems at the front.

Once I reached the hefty bush, I got on my elbows and knees and began army crawling underneath it. A few feet in, I recognized the space we had hollowed out and tucked myself inside. Ella and Margot weren't far behind, spitting dirt out of their mouths as they crawled in beside me. Strands of hair fell out of my braid, but I quickly brushed them away, trying to tuck them back into my beanie.

"Twenty-five, twenty-four, twenty-three..." my one good ear barely picked up the distant counting, and I folded my knees in tighter. Margot had curled her tiny body into a complete ball, barely even recognizable as a human.

"Okay, flashlights off," Ella stated. We all hushed ourselves, the only sound coming from the faraway numbers being yelled out.

My chest heaved with anticipation as I stuck my head between my knees, trying to be as small as possible.

"Three, two, one..." The counters' voices got louder as they counted down the last three numbers.

"Here we come!" I heard one of the counters scream from base. The familiar sound of feet crunching the ground filled the air as the counters spread out, their flashlights beaming into the sandy forested hills. The ocean was a quiet roar in the background, nearly drowned out by the thumping of my heart. When it felt like the footsteps were far away, I dared to lift my eyes up. Ella raised her head at the same time, her eyes meeting mine. She grinned.

"They're going the opposite way. Let's go to base," I muttered, tapping Margot on the shoulder. She was staring the other direction, toward the off-limits Thicket, which was just feet ahead of us.

"What is it?" I asked, following her line of sight. Even though my eyes had adjusted to the darkness by now, it was hard to make out anything other than the shapes of trees, especially from under the bush.

"N-nothing. I just thought I saw–" Margot's stuttering whisper was cut off as footsteps sounded nearby. All of us whipped our heads down and curled back into the fetal position, praying we weren't loud enough to be caught. We were tucked into a giant bush, so I highly doubted anyone would be able to find us, but the counters were often determined.

"I think I heard something over here!" Peyton's unmistakable voice chimed out, followed by her flashlight beam hitting the bush next to us. Margot, Ella, and I were still as stones, barely breathing, not moving, hoping she'd move on. I breathed a sigh of relief as Peyton seemed to turn away, interested in a different sound that caught her attention. I hoisted myself onto my elbows and knees again, giving the girls the silent nod that it was time to run to base.

We army-crawled quietly back out of the prickly undergrowth, making it onto the path that ran adjacent to base. I could nearly see the wooden post, which was about twenty-five feet away.

"Ready?" I whispered over my shoulder.

Margot nodded and Ella signaled for me to start moving. I placed one foot in front of the other, thankful the trees were blocking the counters from seeing us straightaway. After a few thoughtful steps, I broke out into a sprint, Ella and Margot on my heels. My breath came out heavy through my mouth as the post got closer and closer, as if taunting me with being almost there. Finally, I slammed my hand down on the wooden beam and cheered, high-fiving Margot and Ella.

"We made it!" Margot yelled.

Kyle stepped out of the shadows and gave us high-fives. "You're the first three back. That's pretty impressive," he said. His smile was the only thing I could see well through the darkness, the whites of his teeth nearly glowing in the moonlight.

After a few more minutes of the counters searching, a handful of people made it to base safely. An even larger number of people had been caught. Kyle finally called out in his booming voice for anyone still hiding to come out so we could reset. A couple stragglers wandered out from their concealed spots, admitting defeat since they didn't run to base. The group switched, so now Ella, Margot, and I were seekers, along with the rest of the group that had hidden first.

The game went on like this for about an hour until we were on our last round. The girls and I were hiding for the final round, which I was pleased with. I often thought I was better at hiding than seeking.

While the seekers started counting down from base, I turned to Ella and Margot.

"Let's try somewhere new."

"Like, new-new? Somewhere we've never hidden before?" Ella asked.

I nodded, chewing my lip thoughtfully.

"I'm thinking in the beech tree that's on the boundary line," I continued.

"That's far away from base. We could easily get caught coming back," Ella countered.

"Why don't we just hide in our first spot, under the bush? It's the best hiding spot!" Margot said excitedly.

I shook my head. "Let's try something new. Come on, the beech tree," I pushed again. The counters were already thirty seconds into counting. We had just over a minute to get there and hide.

"Fine. But only because it's the last round," Ella gave in, tugging Margot's hand as we trudged through the dune grass toward the large beech tree. The grass was tall enough to whip my waist, but I luckily was protected through layers of clothing. I shone my flashlight directly ahead of us on the wide branches spreading out from the trunk.

"Let's climb a few branches up, just high enough to where they won't see us if they look up there. Then we'll climb down and make our way to base," I said, already sticking my toe into the wood and hoisting myself up, flashlight in mouth.

"Be careful, it's harder to climb in the dark," I heard Ella whisper to Margot as they made their way up the thick branches. After I ascended high enough, I settled with my back against the trunk and my knees pulled up to my chest. Ella was on a branch the same height as me on the opposite side of the trunk. Margot tucked in below me, putting her hood up over her hat to keep the chill out.

I heard the counters reach "one," followed again by their pummeling footfalls and urgent whispering. Through the beech leaves, I saw a pair of girls break off from the other seekers and head toward our tree.

"They're coming. Just be as small as you can and keep your head down," I whisper-called down to Margot. The two teenagers ended up right at the base of our tree shortly after my warning.

"I opened my eyes a little while counting and thought I saw a few girls come this way," one of them said. I had to hold back my scoff.

Cheaters.

A flashlight beam shone up through the branches and I quickly held my breath, pressing my back against the tree until the bark dug into my spine, even through my thick layers. I was fairly certain we were far enough up that the branches below would conceal us, along with our dark clothing.

"Hmm, I'm not seeing anything. Besides, who would be dumb enough to climb up there? They'd never make it to base in time since it would take a while to climb down," the other teenage girl said, her voice whiny and shrill.

"Fine, you're probably right. Let's go this way," the first girl snapped, turning back and going higher up the hill. I waited until they were out of earshot before pulling myself away from the trunk.

"That was close. Let's go. We don't have much time to make it back," Ella said, swinging her legs down to the branch below her. Margot and I followed suit, making as little noise as possible before hitting the ground with a soft thump.

"The fastest way to base is going through that patch of forest," I said, pointing ahead of us.

We all crouched down, the tall greenery concealing us.

"But it's even darker there. We'd have to use our flashlights, and then we'd get caught," Ella responded, shaking her head at me.

"We won't use our flashlights. Trust me. I can get us through it," I shot back.

Ella held my stare for a moment before nodding.

"Lead the way."

All three of us crouched with our heads down, hoods up, as we groveled to the patch of forest. We arrived at the edge of it, and I stood up carefully, making sure no seekers were nearby. I carefully placed one foot onto the spongy forest floor, thankful it was thick enough in there that we weren't noticeably in anyone's view.

I squinted, trying to picture the route we'd take back. I'd only been in this part of the forest a handful of times. It wasn't even really a "forest," more like a patch of trees and thick grass at the base of the dunes.

I clasped Ella's hand in mine and Ella grabbed Margot so we would all stay together. I moved forward but quickly tripped over a large rock.

"Shit."

"Just keep going. You good?" Ella asked.

I nodded and pulled her forward, crouching again as I noticed Ella's eyes widen. She mouthed to me that people were nearby. They were close, but not close enough for us to be worried.

"We're not that far from base. We just need to get through this patch and past the ditch, then we're home free," I whispered.

The three of us trailed along, trying desperately not to get tripped up by rocks or tree roots. Base was nearly visible now. Excitement coursed through me. We could make it back and win. I was about to take another step when a searing bright light shone in my face, jolting me back a few steps. I quickly put my hand over my eyes. The flashlight beam lowered a little, so I dropped my hand, only to swiftly grab Ella's wrist again. Christian stood in front of us, clad in a dark raincoat and black sweats, holding a small flashlight that he now pointed down at the ground.

"Caught you."

CHAPTER 9

I gripped Ella's wrist harder and felt her shove Margot behind her.

"I didn't know you knew about flashlight tag." My voice quavered, even though I wanted to exude confidence. Christian looked at me pitifully before answering.

"I heard about it through the grapevine, thought I'd see what all the excitement was about."

What does he want? So much for our deal for him to leave us alone.

I briefly thought through my options. We were close enough to base that I could call out for Kyle. But what would I say? I didn't even know why Christian was there. He might be there to play, just like us. Adults often joined in on the game. I was surprised I hadn't seen him earlier, though. My mind filled with suspicion, my gut coiling with dread. We were in a dark patch of trees, alone, with our unfamiliar campsite neighbor. Christian took a step backwards, beckoning for us to come with him.

"I caught you, so you're out," he insisted, moving back again. I eyed him warily, assessing every move he made.

"Come on, sugar. Follow the rules," he continued, reaching his hand out to me as he stepped back again, his eyes fixed on us.

Rules? No rule says once you're caught, the seeker has to escort you back to base.

"Come with–" Christian's statement was abruptly cut off as he wailed and fell with a thwack, his flashlight landing on the forest floor.

"He fell into the ditch," Ella said, staring ahead as Christian struggled to stand up in the deep hole, cursing under his breath. I glanced at Ella and Margot, standing behind me still, eyes filled with concern. Then I looked back at Christian, who had now propped himself up and was climbing out.

"Let's go. Just leave him," I decided, sprinting straight through the last few trees and to base. I slammed my hand against the wooden post. Ella and Margot hit it right after I did, their eyes wild and frantic.

Kyle's voice called out, "Impressive! You made it back to base again!"

I nodded, immediately eyeing the ditch where Christian had fallen. What had he been trying to have us do? Did he just want us to admit he caught us? He had done nothing wrong, but it was downright creepy that he had shown up out of nowhere.

"Kyle, did a man join part-way through the game? Brown hair, dark eyes, probably in his thirties?" I asked, tilting my head up at him. Confused, Kyle shook his head and crossed his arms.

"Not that I saw. No one joined after our original group, and I've been standing here the whole time. Unless they came through a different way. Why?"

"Never mind. But I think someone fell into the ditch. He may need help," I said, gesturing to the hole. We all walked over and looked down into the steep dirt pit. My heart started pounding in my chest, and I clenched my fists. Kyle patted my shoulder.

"Good looking-out, kid, but no one's there. They must have continued on playing after they fell."

As Kyle's footsteps faded away, I gaped down at the empty hole.

"Where did he go?" Margot nudged me.

"Probably back to his campsite," I said, stuffing my hands in my pockets. "The better question is," I continued, my voice filling with worry, "why was he here in the first place?"

•　　•　　•　　•　　•

Ella, Margot, and I hiked our way back to our campsite in near silence with our heads down and flashlights on.

"Do we tell our parents he was there?" Margot asked, her hand gripping mine tightly.

I pursed my lips together, considering this.

"I don't know. It seemed like he was there to play, like we were," Ella spoke softly.

"But how did he get there without Kyle seeing him? He must've come a different way. Maybe he didn't want to be seen," I pointed out.

"Maybe he just didn't know the way there. We've been doing it for years. He may have heard about it late and wanted to show up but took a different path," Ella shot back. Even with her defending him, I could tell Christian had spooked us all. If he hadn't fallen in that ditch, I wasn't sure what would have happened next.

There was a warm glow pouring from our campsite as we walked up. The fire was alight, its flames dancing against the night sky, sending sparks flying and crackling into the cold air. My parents sat with Larry and Amy around the fire, talking amongst themselves and laughing. Coach lay at Mom's feet, clearly in a deep sleep.

"Look who's back! How was it?" Amy stood up and wrapped the blanket tighter around her body before repositioning herself back into her camp chair. I faintly heard Margot telling everyone that we made it back to base a handful of times, but my attention was focused elsewhere. Christian sat comfortably in his blue camping chair, holding a beer. A small fire blazed in front of him. I noticed he wasn't wearing the same clothes as minutes earlier at flashlight tag. Now, he wore a gray hoodie with navy sweats. Christian noticed me staring and held up his beer bottle, flashing me a grin. I rolled my eyes and stomped over to where Mom was sitting by the fire, plopping down next to her.

"You okay, sweetie? Margot said you guys got to base quite a few times! And sounds like you caught some people while you were counters, too." Coach woke up and began giving my hand gentle licks.

I sighed. "Mom, did Christian ever leave his campsite tonight?"

Mom's eyes narrowed, and she quickly glanced over my shoulder to where our neighbor sat drinking his beer.

"Honestly, I'm not sure. I didn't pay attention. Why? Should I be worried?" She sped up her words at the end, becoming flustered.

Of course she gets worried now when she thinks something has happened, I thought, feeling my irritation brimming.

Yet, I didn't want to bother her with it, the embarrassing memory of expressing concern about a strange man, only to have it be nothing halted me. After a few moments, I turned to her and took her hand in mine, trying to sound assuring.

"Sorry, no. Everything's fine. Margot's right. We won a few times. I think we're going to head to the bathroom to brush our teeth in a second," I said, squeezing her hand in mine. My mother gave me a knowing look, as if she suspected something else were bothering me.

"Amy and I are also heading to the bathroom in a minute. We'll walk with you."

CHAPTER 10

I stood next to Ella, brushing my teeth fervently and gazing at myself in the dirty bathroom mirror.

"Guess what?" Margot's voice came out garbled, her toothbrush going back and forth in her mouth.

"What?" Ella asked after spitting into the sink.

"Mom said I can sleep with you guys tonight!"

Ella and I exchanged a look. She seemed annoyed, as sometimes big sisters are when their little sisters butt in. Before she could make a snide remark, I spoke up. "Well, that's great, but be prepared to have Coach snuggle up against you. He doesn't know what personal space is."

Margot wrinkled her nose and laughed, spitting out her toothpaste.

"That's fine, I like snuggling with dogs," she said happily. We zipped up our toiletry bags and opened the heavy bathroom door, finding Amy and Mom waiting outside.

"You waited for us?" I asked. Only one trip caused Mom to walk me everywhere—the same time I had lost her trust, the time I cried wolf. That year, a creepy man with a really young girl, who he claimed was his daughter, had been camped near the bathroom. Even the memory made me shudder.

I opened the heavy bathroom door, exiting the small, dank area. Crinkling my nose, I stepped outside and immediately breathed the fresh, crisp air, grateful to be out of the stagnant bathroom.

"Willow!" Ella's voice rang out from a nearby tree outside the bathroom, where she hung upside-down on a branch, her hair cascading nearly to the ground. Margot sat on a branch below her, grinning a toothy smile. I galloped over and swung myself up into the tree, quickly climbing my way up.

"Hi, excuse me?"

I peered below me, realizing the tree we had climbed was sitting directly next to someone's campsite. A fit, young man stared up at me from the tree base. He had sparkling green eyes and dark hair. A friendly smile was plastered on his face.

"Sorry, we didn't know we were in your campsite. We'll get down," I said, dropping myself down one creaky branch at a time.

"Oh, no worries. I actually was just wondering how long you guys are going to be camping here."

I shot Ella a stern look. At fourteen, we knew the seriousness of strangers asking personal questions. It was best to give a vague answer.

"We're usually here for a few days," Ella said confidently, understanding my silent message.

The man gave us a brisk nod then frowned, as if unhappy with our response.

"What's wrong?" Margot's innocent five-year-old voice cut through the air. I inwardly groaned.

"Oh, nothing. I just have my daughter here with me and was hoping she could find a playmate." He gestured behind him where a small, brunette girl with pin straight hair stared at the ground. I hadn't even noticed the child until he pointed her out. I assessed her briefly, thinking how sad she looked. How...uncomfortable she looked.

"We can play with her!" Margot squealed, jumping down from the tree and rushing over. Ella was right behind her, swiftly grabbing her younger sister's arm and tugging her away.

"What she meant to say was, we're sorry, but we have to get back to our campsite now," Ella explained.

I dropped down from a low branch onto the soft dirt, brushing moss and bark off my pants. I gave the man an apologetic nod, following Margot and Ella as we trekked back to our campsite. The man simply stood there, tightly clutching his child's hand. The girl had yet to meet our eyes. Having not fully seen her face, I couldn't even tell her eye color.

As Margot skipped back into our campsite, I saw Amy's face etched with worry.

"You girls were gone a long time just going to the bathroom."

"Some man asked us to play with his daughter," Ella said, cutting right to the chase.

"What man?" Mom appeared from around the car, a dish towel thrown over her shoulder. I nodded and briefly explained what had happened.

"Is that the guy who's camped next to the restrooms? He seemed harmless enough." But Mom paused. After seeing my clear annoyance at her disregard for my feelings, she added, "But let's be careful around him, okay? We'll keep our eyes out for anything strange."

Amy sighed, her eyes darting around. "Let's just try to steer clear of him."

The next morning, we all sat at the picnic table, eagerly munching on our breakfast. Larry had already eaten four pieces of bacon, Dad not far behind him at three. Margot played around with her blueberry pancake using her fork, giggling as she made a mess. I threw my head back in laughter as she smashed a blueberry against her forehead, causing purple and blue juices to roll down her face.

"Hi, excuse me?"

I was startled at the familiar voice coming from the outskirts of our campsite. I turned around and my heart dropped. The odd man with his daughter stood by Dad's car, his dark hair gelled back, and his face cleanly shaven.

"Yes?" Amy called out, displeasure dripping from her voice.

"I'm sorry. I have to run an errand, and I was hoping I could drop my daughter off with you. Her name is Natalie," *the man spoke with an air of superiority, as if he wouldn't take "no" for an answer. He gently pushed his daughter forward. She was wearing a black zip-up jacket, jeans with dirt stains on them, and ratty tennis shoes. She wouldn't meet anyone's eyes.*

"Um, I'm sorry, but you don't even know us," *Mom said. Her eyebrows were raised high with suspicion.*

"I know your girls well enough. Anyway, thanks! See you later, sugar." The man gave his daughter an awkward pat on the back before turning on his heel.

"Wait! What's your name?" Amy called out, throwing up her hands in frustration.

The man ran a hand gently over his gelled hair before flashing a cocky smile.

"Daniel."

"Yep. We just wanted to make sure you were safe," Mom said, eyeing me.

We fell in step together as we strolled back to the campsite. As we passed Christian's campsite, I noticed his fire was dwindling and he was nowhere in sight.

What if he's hiding somewhere and watching us? Hopefully he just went to bed.

"Okay, Margot is sleeping with you guys tonight. I trust you girls not to stay up too late," Amy said with a wink. I grabbed my hoodie off the chair where Dad still sat.

"You guys aren't going to bed?" I wondered, my gaze shifting between Larry and Dad, both seated at the campfire which blazed on.

"Just thought we'd stay up a little longer while all the ladies went to sleep," Larry said matter-of-factly, taking a drink of his sparkling water. Dad stood up and went to the car, rifling around the seats for something. I turned back to Larry.

"Did Mom say something to you guys?" I asked, putting my hands on my hips.

"Just that she wanted us to watch over everyone for a bit. You know how moms are, they worry," Larry said, his smile not quite reaching his eyes.

Out of the corner of my eye, I peered at my parents' tent, which was unzipped. Mom sat on the air mattress, deep in conversation with Dad, who now stood just outside of it. I watched as he handed something to her, whispering to her urgently. Mom nodded and took the item, which was too far away for me to see, then zipped the tent up. As Dad strolled back over, I couldn't help myself. "What was that about?" I tilted my head toward their tent.

Dad swung his arm around me and squeezed affectionately. "I was just giving your mom her phone; she left it at the picnic table. Also, here's *your* phone. She still had it from when you went off to flashlight tag."

He slid me the black device, and I pocketed it.

"Okay, well, looks like everyone is going to bed but you and Larry." I drew my words out, hoping he would tell me why the adults were acting so weird. Dad pressed a kiss against my head. I saw Amy reach down and hug her husband before climbing into the Grisham's red tent, which, unfortunately, was placed just a few feet away from Christian's.

"Don't worry about Larry and me. We're just having some catch-up time while you girls get your beauty rest. Keep an eye on Margot, will you? She's excited to sleep in your tent tonight."

I gave him and Larry a sidelong look before making my way over to Ella's and my tent. Coach sat patiently outside, his small nub of a tail wagging as I got closer.

"Let's go to bed, bud," I murmured, unzipping the tent. Ella and Margot were already inside, Margot sitting criss-cross applesauce on top of her sleeping bag.

"Time to tell scary stories!" The lanky eight-year-old threw her arms out for dramatic effect, imitating a zombie. I frowned, my own frightening thoughts clouding my mind. I couldn't get the image of Christian's face when he cornered us out of my head. Because it was creepy, yes, but something else was bothering me. When he stood there, with that arrogant smirk on his face, it tickled something in my brain. Something about him was almost familiar to me, maybe even triggering. Whether it was the crook of his nose, the conceited look on his face, or his messy brown hair, I wasn't sure. What was I missing? He didn't look like anyone I knew.

"Excuse me?"

The startling snap of Ella's fingers in front of my face jolted me out of my petrifying contemplation.

I grimaced before apologizing. "Sorry. I got lost in my thinking. Please, Margot, tell your spooky story."

After over thirty minutes of Margot and Ella competing for the best harrowing tale, my eyes began to droop. Coach lay happily at my feet, snoring softly. We were completely in the dark, but my eyes had adjusted. I could make out the outline of Ella's frizzy hair and Margot's dramatic hand gestures.

A voice suddenly penetrated the air. It came from outside our tent, but it wasn't loud enough for me to decipher words. Margot continued with her story, oblivious to the noise.

"And then the ghost said–"

"Shh, Margot. I thought I heard something." Ella put a finger to her lips to urge us to quiet down. I quickly checked my phone; it was almost midnight. The campground had designated quiet hours that started at 10 p.m.

Another voice shouted out, closer this time.

"That sounded like...your dad," Ella whispered. Before I could respond, Coach shot up out of his sleep and forced his nose into the base of the zipper that closed our tent.

"Coach, wait!" I screamed. It was too late—the intelligent dog had escaped the tent. Margot, Ella, and I were frozen in place, the flaps of our now partially open tent whistling in the wind. After a few seconds, my good ear picked up on Coach's angry bark, followed by Larry, who yelled, "Sit down, for God's sake!"

My hands trembled, but I managed to unzip the tent the rest of the way, and we held back the front flap. My chest was heaving even more than it had been at flashlight tag, and I struggled to take in enough air.

In through your nose. Out through your mouth. I attempted to slow my panicked breathing.

We all peered out. Carefully. Cautiously. Hesitantly.

The first thing I glimpsed was Mom, standing outside my parents' tent. She held something in her hands, but she was too far away for me to discern what the object was. It must be heavy because she used both hands to clutch it tightly. Coach stood in front of her protectively, and I didn't need to be close to know he was on edge. The Grisham's red tent was unzipped partially at the bottom, the tent door flap ajar. Ella grabbed my arm and squeezed it tight.

"Willow, look."

My eyes followed to where she pointed with her other hand. Immediately, all the hairs in my body stood up, goosebumps covering every inch of my skin.

Dad and Larry stood together with their arms crossed, staring down at Christian, who was sitting back at his campsite in his chair with an aloof look on his face just visible by the firelight. He hoisted himself out of the chair when Larry grabbed both his shoulders and shoved him back into the seat. I gasped, perhaps a little too loudly, since Larry and both my parents turned their heads toward me, as if just now realizing we were awake watching. Margot began to shake behind me, and Ella instinctively wrapped her arms tightly around her, fear filling her face.

"W-what's happening?" I called out, hoping any of the adults would answer me.

Christian began to mumble something, and Dad whipped his head around, anger seething out of him as he spit out his next words. "Don't even look at them."

I opened my mouth to repeat my question when Amy warily poked her head out from her tent.

"What in the *hell* is going on?" she yelled, exasperated.

Larry whispered in Dad's ear then joined Amy outside their tent, leaving Dad in front of our strange neighbor. Amy seemed bewildered, confusion filling her face. While Larry began talking to his wife quietly, Dad kept his eyes glued on Christian. After a moment, my father spoke softly to my mother, almost eerily, as if one small thing could tip him over the edge.

"Eve. Go to the kids."

Mom shuffled toward us, Coach right on her heels. As she drew near, my jaw dropped open.

"Mom, is that a *gun*?"

The sleek black object in her hand was unmistakable.

My mother was holding a pistol.

CHAPTER 11

"Yes, it's a gun, Willow. Listen to me. We're probably going to need to call the police soon." Mom said.

Confused, I found myself nodding, even though my brain was processing none of the information.

"Larry and your dad stayed awake tonight because they had a weird feeling. Sometimes, you can't explain it. Plus, I was worried after you asked me if Christian had left his campsite during flashlight tag." Mom's lip quivered as she whispered to us quietly.

I felt Ella shift beside me uncomfortably, her gaze focused on Dad and Christian, who hadn't moved. They may be close enough to at least hear some of what Mom was explaining, as there was only one campsite separating us. She took a deep breath before continuing.

"Just a few minutes ago, your dad heard rustling behind him, and he shone his flashlight around. He found…" she trailed off, as if contemplating how to word the next part.

"What did he find?" Margot's wobbly voice made me want to wrap her in my arms.

"He found Christian…but Christian was on his hands and knees, with his hood up. And he was…he was climbing into your mother's tent."

I was silent as I let the news sink in.

"Are you saying he was trying to …" Ella paused and glanced at Margot, choosing her words carefully. "Are you saying he was trying to secretly get into my parent's tent and…*hurt* Mom?"

My heart beat rapidly, sweat forming on my forehead despite the chilly night. I could decipher the haunted look on Mom's face. It was worse than what Ella suggested.

"Well, honey, it's a bit of a crazy night, what with Margot sleeping with you two tonight." She raised her eyebrows at me, clearly trying to subtly communicate without words.

I gasped, horror filling my stomach, spreading out and overwhelming my senses. She meant Christian's target was probably Margot.

"Do you mean …?" Ella asked, her eyes as wide as mine. Mom nodded imperceptibly.

Margot was too young to understand what Mom was implying or the true severity of it, but the intensity of the situation frightened her. Tears flowed from her eyes, and she buried her face in her older sister's shoulder.

"Okay, okay. Well, why do you have the gun?" I stumbled over my words, desperately trying to make sense of the situation. My shaky breaths were causing puffs of air in the cold night.

Mom inhaled deeply and shifted the pistol to one hand, petting Coach's head with the other. The dog still stood by her, but his gaze was pinned on Christian.

"Well, Larry grabbed Christian out of the tent and nearly dragged him back into his own campsite. He shoved him into his camping chair and told him to stay put. Your dad left the gun with me earlier, and honey, you know we have our concealed weapons permit. He told me to keep it by my pillow until he came to bed, just in case. He–"

"Hold on," I interrupted. "You and dad may have your permits, but I've never seen you bring your gun camping with you."

My parents obtained their permits years ago, and they recently made me take a class on gun safety, where I was taught how to properly handle and shoot a gun. Although I was aware there were guns in the house, I had never noticed them bring one anywhere outside of the house.

A small smile crept onto Mom's face. "Actually, that's a story for another time. But, you're right. This is the first year we brought a gun with us. Call it...fate, I guess." She shrugged. Margot's sobs subsided slightly, and Mom reached out instinctively to rub her back.

"Sweetie, we would never let Christian get to you." She quickly added, "Or to any of you, any of us." I could tell she was flustered, having explained more than she intended to. Margot's eyes became glassy, and I thought she might start crying again. I didn't blame her.

Appearing resigned with the whole situation, Mom said, "I only told you so you understand how serious this is. Unfortunately, looking back, we think he kept engaging with us over the last couple days to get close and watch you girls. Tonight, I think he decided to take it a step further. Thank God Nick heard him trying to get into the tent," she said, her eyes widening.

"W-would he have k-kidnapped me?" Margot's shaky voice implored as she clutched Ella's jacket.

"Margot, if he had even laid a finger on you, we would have caught him faster than you can blink," I said reassuringly, patting her leg. Margot's youthful exuberance was gone, her face ashen. This was a lot to hear for Ella and me, but I couldn't imagine being Margot's age and trying to understand what had nearly happened tonight.

Mom grabbed my leg from where she crouched outside the tent, and I shifted my attention back to her. "There is a reason I am being so truthful and telling you what happened tonight. I don't mean to scare any of you girls, especially not Margot, but I needed you to understand how truly dangerous this man is. Do you guys hear me?"

I didn't know if I had ever seen such an intense, heated look in my mother's eyes before. Right then, with her right hand gripping the sleek black gun and her other hand grasping my pajama pants, her eyes aglow with what could only be called a mother's protection, she looked untouchable. Perhaps the strongest I had ever seen her. With just one look at her, I knew she would rather shoot Christian than let him touch any of us. A surge of pride pumped through my veins as I covered her hand with mine.

"I hear you."

"You're wrong about me, you know." Christian's voice felt like claws ripping through my scalp, forcing me to acknowledge that he still sat a short distance away, Dad hovering over him.

"Shut. Your. Mouth." Dad enunciated the words slowly, flitting his eyes briefly over to us before settling back on the menacing man in front of him.

Christian appeared to have lost all emotion because he gave Dad a wide, arrogant smile that didn't reach his eyes before saying, "You didn't listen. You're. Wrong. I'm not some child molester."

Dad crouched down until his eyes were level with Christian's. I watched intently as Dad formed his words. "If you so much as move a muscle from this chair, my wife will shoot you on the spot. We'll call it self-defense. Try me."

For a moment, I thought Christian was going to bite out a snarky response, but heavy silence filled the crisp night air. Amy rushed over and grabbed Margot in her arms. I expected tearful words and an emotional exchange since Larry had just caught her up, but Amy just pulled Margot quickly back from the hug and stared at her.

"He won't touch you. I promise."

"Mom, he almost got into *your* tent. Not ours." Her squeaky voice now had a hint of playfulness in it, thankfully.

"You were supposed to be there with me tonight. He...he could have..." Now, tears leaked from Amy's eyes as the gut-wrenching realization truly hit her. Mom put her arm around her friend, fiercely comforting her.

Ella's gaze switched from her mom, to the firepit, to Christian before settling on Amy again. She chewed her lip worriedly, as if deciding on her next words. Finally, she opened her mouth, her statement coming out in one big rush.

"This is very poor timing. But I desperately have to pee."

CHAPTER 12

After a few hushed words between both sets of parents, it was decided that Larry would accompany Margot, Ella, and I on the short walk to the bathroom. Dad, Amy, and Mom would stay behind and keep an eye on Christian. Since the adrenaline of it all had died down a little, Margot and I had realized that our bladders felt full as well.

I placed my hood up, trying to warm my ears. It was very late at night, or perhaps even early in the morning, and near-silence filled the campground. I could barely hear the crash of ocean waves and a baby crying in the distance, but otherwise, the only sound I could make out was my own heavy breathing mixed with Margot and Ella's. We walked quickly with our heads down and Larry behind us. His head was on a swivel, and as I glanced over my shoulder at him, I realized he was wearing his usual ankle holster with his own gun. I had forgotten about it in all the chaos, but Larry was always protected. He wore his ankle holster like it was his second skin. And similar to a snake, he never shed his second skin unless necessary.

Comfort washed through me, filling my veins with warmth. It's not that I was a huge gun supporter, but knowing we had some protection against what turned out to be a very dangerous man was a relief.

As I turned my head back around, the desolate bathroom building came into view. The lights outside the building were on, so I turned my phone flashlight off and stuck it into my hoodie pocket. One of the lights toward the corner of the building was flickering, adding an eerie glow to our surroundings.

Larry nodded to us, sticking his hands in his jean pockets.

"I'll be waiting out here for you," he told us solemnly.

Margot chose the stall nearest to the flickering light, the door thudding loudly as it shut behind her. Ella quickly went into the next stall. I gave an uneasy glance to Larry before I chose the right-hand bathroom. As the heavy door closed behind me, I locked it hurriedly.

Although having Larry on watch helped calm my nerves, I kept feeling dread creep into the pit of my stomach. What Christian had done was terrifying, and I had the strange sense it wasn't close to being resolved. Even if we called the cops now, what were we to say? Christian hadn't actually crawled fully into the tent when Dad caught him, and he surely hadn't been able to reach Amy before he was dragged out into his chair. The cops couldn't arrest someone for "nearly" breaking and entering, even if it seemed like he had dark intentions.

I briefly had the impending feeling that the four dirty bathroom walls were closing in on me.

In through your nose. Out through your mouth.

The deep breathing technique was usually a quick fix unless a true panic attack was coming. I completed a few more inhales and exhales before admitting to myself that the panicky feeling was rising, not falling. Despite the cool chill of the air under the bathroom door, I felt sweat bead on my forehead. A steady, pounding rhythm began in my chest, and I exhaled a shaky breath.

I was about to have a panic attack.

Tears formed in the corners of my eyes, but I couldn't focus enough to wipe them away. I gripped the bathroom sink, still trying to get enough oxygen into my lungs.

In through your nose. Hold for five seconds. Out through your mouth.

The old trick wasn't doing a great job. My heart felt like it was beating so hard against my chest that it would explode, leaving a scarred hole in my body cavity where it used to be.

I'm going to die.

This was often one of my thoughts during a panic attack. I began having these episodes just in the last few months, likely brought on by the stress of applying to college and my parent's arguments. I knew how the attacks usually ended, and it wasn't pretty.

The white porcelain sink and grimy drain were all I could make out through my blurred, teary vision. The knot that had formed in my stomach earlier grew stronger and sharper, and I let out a soft sob.

No, not here. Not now.

As the knot became too painful to ignore, mixed with my rapid, irregular heartbeats, I gave in to what I thought my body wanted. I bent over the sink and dry-heaved several times, terrible choking sounds filling the dismal bathroom. My face now wet with tears, I gathered myself enough to wipe them off. How long had I been here now? A few minutes? I placed a hand on my chest and inhaled strongly, finally feeling the tension in my chest and stomach begin to crumble and ease. More than I hated dry-heaving, I absolutely despised the attacks coming out of nowhere. I hated that my body thought this was the only way to get the pounding anxiety to go away. I unlocked the door after I felt my body relax a little more and swung it open, trying to formulate an excuse for why I had taken so long.

I breathed in the frigid air, closing my eyes and reveling in its freshness. When I opened them, a pang of horror hit me again. Margot and Ella stood next to each other, shivering, a frightened look on both their faces.

Larry was gone.

The three of us hurriedly eyed each other and simply stood in place, as if frozen in time, paralyzed amongst whatever night-out-of-a-horror-film this was. As my hazel eyes surveyed Ella's green ones, I was transported back in time, my memories wracking my thoughts.

As Daniel walked urgently away from our campsite, my eyes instantly connected with Ella's. She shrugged her shoulders at me, both of us undeniably confused by the strange "daughter" Daniel had dropped off. The young girl's pin straight hair we had seen just a day before was now frizzy and untamed, and her eyes were cast downward, fixated on her feet. She held a worn stuffed tiger in the crook of her left arm. I shifted my gaze from her long enough to see Mom murmuring worriedly to Amy, their heads tilted together and backs turned to us. The child, apparently called Natalie, still perched at the edge of our campsite, not uttering a word. Margot dropped her fork onto her plate with a clatter and scooted off the picnic table bench. She dusted herself off and wiped her forehead for a few seconds to rid herself of the blueberry stain before tromping directly over to Natalie and extending her hand.

"Natalie, I'm Margot. We're having blueberry pancakes for breakfast. Do you want to join us?"

Mom and Amy both whipped their heads around quickly, apprehension etched into the lines of their faces. Amy opened her mouth to interrupt, but my mother gently laid a hand on her arm. Larry and Dad sat silently across from each other at the picnic table next to us, waiting with bated breath for the child's next move.

But Natalie didn't budge.

She didn't move an inch. Margot, being only five years old with no filter, tilted her head down so she was looking up into Natalie's eyes, which were still fixed firmly on the dirt.

"You don't have to be scared of us."

My heart cracked at Margot's sweet, innocent voice. She and Ella were brought up in a house where you sat with the lonely kid at lunch or you offered a homeless man your food. I was raised with similar morals, so I understood Margot trying to reach this girl, who couldn't have been older than Margot herself.

But Natalie, yet again, didn't take the bait. I had never seen a child stand so still for so long. My gut twisted, dread coiling in the pit of my stomach like a viper waiting to strike. Something was wrong.

Margot finally shrugged her shoulders and skipped back to the table, calling out, "Fine, more pancakes for us, then!"

Mom crouched down next to Natalie then, softly whispering to her and attempting to comfort her. She rubbed her back and tried to grasp her hand, but Natalie continued to stare at her own shoes. Mom lifted her head, an exasperated look on her face.

"Eve, just let her come over on her own when she's ready," Amy said, motioning for Mom to come back with her to eat breakfast. As my mother walked toward the rest of us, now all seated at the table quietly finishing our

food, Ella gasped. I whipped around, realizing that Natalie had lifted her head.

Blue. Her eyes were blue. I breathed a sigh of relief, hoping she was now feeling comfortable enough to join us for some pancakes, but the relief was short-lived. We collectively stared as Natalie steadily lifted her right arm, pointing directly behind us. She didn't utter a word. Her feet planted firmly on the ground, hair unkempt, and left arm still clutching her stuffed tiger, she determinedly pointed behind us.

I turned my head, an uneasy feeling settling in my bones, and followed the direction of her small finger.

She was pointing to the Thicket.

CHAPTER 13

"Nine-one-one."

"What?" I immediately shook the peculiar memory off, alarmed by Ella's words.

"I asked if you had your phone. I think we need to call 911," my best friend repeated. I detected a slight quiver in her otherwise steady voice. Margot leaned her head closer to Ella's shoulder, nestling into her in fear.

"W-where did your dad go?" My own voice was trembling. I looked around, but the building lights only illuminated a few feet ahead of us. I could barely make out the outline of other tents and RVs, could barely view the dark trees blowing in the vengeful wind. I wished the soft rush of the ocean waves could drown out my pounding thoughts.

"We came out of the bathroom right before you, but Dad was running back toward our campsite. We thought we heard yelling..." Ella trailed off as muffled shouts arose again through the normally quiet campground.

The yelling was too far away to hear clearly, especially for me, but it was loud enough to know it was Dad's voice. Margot clenched the hem of her jacket in her fist, her eyes becoming as wide as saucers. Ella's words came out firmer this time.

"I think you need to call 911. We didn't bring our phones with us, but you did. You have to call."

I nodded, pulling my device from my sweatshirt pocket. As the screen lit up, I barely noticed it was 1:14 a.m. or that my battery was at 25%. My hands shook fiercely as I pulled up the phone app.

"Ella, my phone has no service," I whispered, staring down at the dot-dot-dot that appeared in the upper right-hand corner of my home screen.

"It should still go through if it's an emergency call."

"I hope you're right."

My thumb hovered above the "9," still trembling uncontrollably from fear and adrenaline. I bit my lip, my heart pounding against my roaring thoughts. I had never needed to call 911 before. I wasn't even sure what to say to the operator. Margot tugged on Ella's sweatshirt gently, murmuring something to her sister.

"What?" Ella sounded slightly irritated, but I assumed it was from all the nerves.

"Ella, w-who is that?" Margot repeated what I'm guessing was her previous whisper to her sister, louder this time.

My finger was hovering over the last "1" on the call screen as I figured out what Margot was referring to. A figure was walking toward us. He was barely visible through the misty haze at the end of the path that led to the bathroom. The starry sky and flickering bathroom lights provided the only sources of visibility we had into the black night. Ella whipped her head back at me furiously. He was coming closer.

"Willow, call *now!*"

I tapped the final "1" quickly as the figure moved closer to us. Margot hiccupped a sob of fear as I held the phone up to my ear, unable to steady it against my anxious tremors. At last, the figure strode into the light, and I nearly collapsed from relief, hitting the "end call" button.

Larry.

"Dad! What the hell! We thought you were Christian! You just took off and left us here then came back without telling us it was you? We couldn't see you!" Even though Ella was viciously spitting her words out at her father, I could detect her slowly relaxing at the sight of him.

However, Larry seemed anything but relaxed. His eyes were wild, and he spoke with urgency. "I'll explain why I left you on our way back to the campsite. We have to head back so Nick can leave."

"Wait, where's my dad going?" I asked.

Larry inhaled deeply, rubbing one hand over his face before answering.

"To get the ranger."

•   •   •   •   •

As we trekked the short walk back to our campsite, Larry explained the situation. When we all had gone into our separate bathroom stalls, Larry heard yelling from our campsite. Worried that Christian had attacked someone, he sprinted back there.

Christian had gotten out of his chair when Mom was momentarily distracted. He approached Dad with his hands in the air, making excuses for his behavior and saying, "I thought I was getting into my own tent earlier, I swear." Dad had told Christian to sit back down before he called the cops, but Christian hadn't listened. Instead, things escalated. He began screaming and flailing his arms, charging at Dad. Mom held up the gun, but Dad and Christian were so close to each other that she didn't have a clear shot. By the time Larry arrived, Christian had shoved my father and was just inches away from his face.

Before Larry could intervene, Coach did.

As soon as Christian laid his hands on Dad's shoulders, Coach reached down and gripped Christian's ankle in his mouth, biting down. Christian yelled and attempted to kick Coach. Larry grabbed Christian by his shirt collar and practically dragged him back into his camping chair, once again.

Larry was flush-faced and nearly breathless as we neared the campsite.

"I've never seen Coach like that. He had spit dripping from his chin and was baring his teeth. He looked like a wolf," Larry said, shoving his hand through his hair.

Light from several lanterns brightened our site enough to see under the EZ-Up. Amy and Mom were seated at the picnic table, their hands wrapped tightly around their mugs. As for what was inside the mugs—coffee, hot chocolate, alcohol—I didn't know, but I wouldn't blame them for whatever it was. It had been a long night, and it wasn't even over.

"You're back." Mom abruptly stood up from the table, reaching out for me. She was no longer holding the pistol, but her whole demeanor screamed distress. I embraced her briefly before pulling back to assess where Dad was. Christian sat in his own campsite on his chair, his head resting idly against his hand. His eyes were glazed over, and he looked bored. A small pool of blood formed by his shoe, trickling down his pant leg. Dad stood in front of him, pistol tucked in the back of his shorts, arms crossed.

"Nick, go on and get the ranger. I'll keep watch, but I'm sure he'll think twice about leaving his chair again after Coach got him," Larry called out.

Coach.

Was he okay? Did Christian hurt him?

Fury rose quick as lightning through my gut until it spilled over into my veins, my head, my heart. In mere moments, I could feel anger seeping from every pore of my body at the thought of someone hurting my dog.

I impulsively wanted to march right over to Christian and swipe the lazy look off his face. My leg twitched impatiently, and I began to get up from the picnic table when I felt something warm brush against my hand. When I glanced down, two chocolate brown eyes stared up at me.

Coach. Safe.

I rubbed my dog's fuzzy ears, relief flooding through me like water, squelching the simmering anger that nearly just burned me up. Coach nudged my feet apart gently, planting himself firmly between my legs. He was guarding me.

The sound of our Ford Expedition's engine starting up rose through the campsite, and I looked over to see Dad leave the car running and jog over to us. He planted a quick kiss on top of Mom's head and slipped her the pistol again so quickly that I hardly caught it.

"Be safe. Don't use this unless you absolutely have to."

Mom's head bobbed once, acknowledging she understood what he meant and was determined to protect our family while he was away. After a few moments, the Expedition noisily clambered down the uneven road, getting farther away from the danger that enveloped us.

I peeked at Christian, whose eyes looked vacant despite the ever-growing pool of blood beneath him. Larry was just a few feet away keeping watch.

I blew a loose, shaky breath out of my mouth. A warm hand on the small of my back interrupted my thoughts, instantly making me feel safer. Mom gently led me to the picnic table where I collapsed next to Amy, Margot, and Ella. Coach immediately took up a vigil at my feet, staring toward Christian's campsite. Each ear swivel indicated him assessing for threat, each rumble in his throat a warning that if that man were to come near us, he was going to do something about it.

Mom held out a blanket for me, which I placed around my shoulders gratefully. The air was chilly, which I hadn't noticed much in the chaos of the eventful evening. Amy offered a blanket to her daughters then stole a glimpse of her husband, who stood determinedly between our campsite and Christian.

"What a night," Mom said softly, gripping her mug in her left hand. I could smell the bitter aroma of coffee, which solved the mystery of what Amy and Mom were drinking. I briefly wondered when they even had the time to make coffee tonight, but my curiosity faltered as Margot spoke up.

"Does anyone want to play Uno?"

After a long pause, Ella laughed. Full-on belly laughed, nearly spitting across the picnic table. Amy soon followed, her eyes brimming with tears as peals of laughter burst forth. Mom and I looked at each other for a brief moment before joining in. Margot giggled as she stared at us with wide eyes, confusion lacing her tone as she asked, "What's so funny?"

I had tears from laughter spilling out as I tried to catch my breath. The mere thought of playing a game amidst the mayhem was absurd. We were monitoring a stranger who tried to climb into Amy's tent while Dad went to find a ranger. However, Margot was young and likely confused about everything happening, so it made total sense she was trying to bring some normalcy into the night. My phone screen brightened, alerting me I only had 18% battery. The time on the screen read 1:39 a.m.

Amy dabbed her eyes with a corner of a blanket before clearing her throat and reaching her hand out to touch her youngest daughter's.

"Yeah, honey, let's play Uno," she said.

CHAPTER 14

Ten minutes later, the low rumbling of our family car rolling into the campsite grabbed everyone's attention, including Christian's. The jerk of his head toward the car told me he was at least slightly nervous about Dad bringing a ranger back with him. Except, no patrol car was following Dad. Mom's eyes found mine for a heartbeat before she tightened her grip on the pistol, which she kept by her side. The Expedition's interior light flicked on as Dad hesitantly exited the vehicle. He dipped his head at Larry, who quickly glanced toward Christian once with his steely eyes before joining everyone at the picnic table. As Larry and Dad settled into the picnic table, Dad lifted his head and gazed at everyone solemnly.

"The kiosk was empty—no ranger," he stated.

"What do you mean, 'no ranger'?" Larry blurted out, keeping his voice low so Christian wouldn't overhear. An overnight ranger was always stationed at the kiosk. Surprisingly, even with nobody guarding him, Christian still positioned himself comfortably in his blue seat. At least he wasn't attempting to come back over to our campsite.

"There's no ranger. There was a sign that said, 'No ranger on duty tonight.' It didn't have an explanation. I don't know where the nearest police station is, and my phone has no service," Dad continued in a hushed tone.

Larry covered his face with his hands in frustration for a moment before grabbing Amy's hand in his. Mom simultaneously reached out for Dad, brushing her hand over his in comfort.

"So, what? We're just going to have to guard him all night?" Mom spoke up. As soon as the words came out, determination filled her gaze.

"We'll guard him all night," she repeated. She wasn't asking a question this time. Her deep brown eyes were locked on Dad, who was clearly thinking through options.

"We could just call the police. Maybe they could escort him out, or station a patrol car by him," Amy suggested. Ella nodded slightly in agreement.

"Ames, as horrible as it was, he didn't actually get the chance to grab you. He never laid hands on you. Nick and I got him out before anything happened. I'm not sure that would 'count' as a crime in the officers' eyes," Larry said gently, his hand still clenching Amy's.

Silence followed Larry's sentence, the terrible reality of what he said settling in. He was right—

technically Christian hadn't done anything, but that certainly didn't mean he hadn't intended to.

Mom must have been reading my mind because she said, "The intention was clear, Larry."

"They don't arrest people based on intentions." Larry's voice raised moderately. I flinched. I was not a fan of conflict.

"You don't have to raise your voice at my wi–"

"Christian's running away!" Margot was out of her seat, tears rimming her eyes. Horrified, everyone turned their gaze to Margot, who was pointing to the Thicket. Christian's body was barely visible in the jet-black night, his camp chair empty, his arms pumping as he raced through the outskirts of the forest beyond. Watching him disappear into the trees reminded me of my earlier memory of Natalie.

I turned my gaze toward the Thicket then, to where Natalie still stood pointing in the direction of the sunlit forest.

Ella whispered in my ear, "Why is she pointing in there?"

I simply shook my head. I thought maybe the young girl had seen something, like a bunny or a raccoon, but the forest revealed nothing out of the ordinary. Lichen draped from the woodland outskirt's tree branches and dune grass shifted in the light wind. Natalie dropped her hand, still silent. Mom and Amy wore confused looks on their faces. No one knew what to do about this odd girl that a stranger dropped off moments before. Natalie wouldn't communicate, other than pointing to the forest.

I had an idea.

"Mom, maybe Natalie wants to go into the forest and play? Maybe that's what she's trying to tell us?" I gave my suggestion hesitantly, unsure if I was reading the stranger correctly.

Mom and Amy exchanged a quick glance, whispering to each other tersely.

"That's fine. All four of you go, though. And please don't go too far. We're in charge of Natalie for the time being, I suppose, so be careful," Amy said, wiping her hands on a dish towel. She nudged Margot forward encouragingly.

"Natalie, are you coming?" I asked as we jogged toward the trees. To everyone's surprise, Natalie nodded and followed behind me, allowing me to lead the way. I shrugged at Mom, who watched us with concerned eyes. Ella, Margot, Natalie, and I hiked through the Thicket single-file, following a worn dirt path. Pine needles crunched under my shoes, and the grass cut my exposed legs, but we finally closed in on a tree I found suitable for climbing. I dug the toe of my shoe into the soft bark and swung my leg over a low-hanging branch, quickly wiping the sap off my hands onto my shorts.

"You took the spot I was going for," Ella whined.

"Find your own spot." I stuck my tongue out at her, giggling.

Soon, Ella and Margot had both claimed places near me on the sturdy tree. Natalie stood not far beneath us, uninterested.

"What's wrong with her?" Margot attempted to whisper, but it came out much too loud.

"Margot, shut up. Maybe she's just shy." Ella reached for her sister and tried to flick her, nearly losing her balance in the process.

"Hey, how cool! We can see the beach parking lot from here," I said excitedly. We were in the middle of the green belt making up the Thicket, with a view of the tops of our tents to one side and the parking lot on the other. This campground had a general lot for people who were visiting the beach for the day. The Thicket was the only thing separating the parking lot from the campground. My eyes roamed the near-empty lot, the dingy bathroom, and the huge sandy hill that led to the roaring ocean. Shifting myself so I could get more comfortable, I looked down and realized Natalie was also staring at the parking area. Picnic tables were scattered around in the distant lot as well, with a man seated at one of them. I frowned, squinting my eyes so I could view him better. He was hunched over the table, appearing to be drawing or writing something. The man lifted his head up after a few moments and met my gaze, smiling.

My stomach dropped.

It was Daniel.

"No!" Amy's scream jolted me out of the memory, and everything came back in a rush as fast and aggressive as an unexpected wave.

Larry was sprinting into the Thicket after Christian, Dad right on his heels.

"Why don't they just let him go?" Ella yelled. Her eyes mirrored her sister's, glassy with tears, out of fear and worry for our dads who were now chasing a predator into the woods.

Maybe even a violent predator.

"If he runs off now, he may come back and catch us by surprise. It's better to know where he is and keep an eye on him." Mom's voice was surprisingly calm as she held onto Amy. Amy cried into Mom's shoulder, her chest heaving as Larry and Dad disappeared into the dark forest.

I reached down below the picnic table and ... Coach wasn't there.

"Mom. Mom! Coach is gone. He must have run after them into the woods." I didn't need to be worried about him, too.

Mom shook her head in disbelief. "He wanted to protect your dad. He'll come back."

My chest instantly tightened. As I felt panic rising in my body, a small hand clasped mine. Margot looked up at me, her penetrating, emerald eyes remarkably bright in the soft lantern's glow.

"Coach will be okay. So will your dad and my dad. They just want to protect us."

The child's gentle words unfortunately did not ease the anxiety trapped in my lungs. I caught the uneasy gaze Mom and Amy exchanged as Margot continued to grasp my hand firmly. I squinted, trying to see through the thick darkness that blanketed the Thicket.

We paced around our site anxiously for twenty minutes that felt like hours, when a noise came from the Thicket. Mom jumped up, biting her fingernails as the ruckus got louder. The first one out of the tall grass was Coach, who came bounding up and licked me all over. I hugged him, grateful he was okay. Both Larry and Dad emerged next, unscathed but angry. Amy rushed up and hugged Larry tightly, while Mom followed suit with Dad.

After releasing Mom, Dad cleared his throat. "He got away."

CHAPTER 15

The early hours of the morning in Westport were simultaneously eerie and calm between the angry crashes of ocean waves and the black sky twinkling with millions of stars. I stared at those stars now, with the sounds of the sea reverberating in my one good ear. My heart had finally slowed about an hour before, although Christian still hadn't resurfaced. It had now been about two hours since he disappeared into the Thicket. None of us had gone to bed.

Well, no one except Margot, since children could sleep through anything.

Amy sat in front of the fire, Margot sprawled out in her lap, both covered by a big, fuzzy blanket. I sat at the picnic table with Larry and Dad, who were engrossed in a cribbage game. As occupied as they were, they kept their heads turning every few minutes in case Christian reappeared. Ella and Mom had joined Amy and Margot in front of the fire. They had their hoods up, eyes fixed on the dancing flames in front of them.

I reached down and scratched Coach's thick neck fur. He hadn't slept either, keeping his gaze forward on the spot where Christian had run off hours ago. My body felt exhausted, the after-effects of adrenaline slowly trickling in.

"What time is it?" I whispered to Dad.

"It's 3:25 a.m.," he said.

I could feel his assessing eyes boring into my skin. "You and Ella should go to your tent. Try to get some sleep while you can," he finally said.

Larry nodded his agreement but said nothing. I groaned and placed my head in my hands. My eyes were drooping. After a few minutes, I noticed Coach's eyes had drifted shut at last.

At least he's getting some sleep.

I knew Dad was right. Even with Christian out there and all of us on alert, I was so physically and emotionally drained that I would likely fall asleep the second my head hit the pillow. I made eye contact with Ella across the campsite and nodded toward our tent.

"Okay, we're going to try to get some sleep. Do you want us to take Margot with us?" I cast a glance toward the sleeping child.

Larry shook his head. "Nah, she's fine out here with us. Just leave her."

I hugged Dad and joined Ella at the entrance of our tent.

"Looks like somebody wants to join us," she said sleepily, pointing behind me. Coach stood loyally behind my legs, waiting patiently for the command to enter.

"C'mon, Coach." I urged.

As soon as I settled into my sleeping bag, with Coach at my feet and Ella by my side, I was asleep.

•　　•　　•　　•　　•

I awoke to screaming. The kind of screaming that hits you in the gut and wakes you so fast you can't even think straight. Ella shot up next to me. Coach was on his feet, his hackles up.

The scream sounded again. I unzipped the tent and allowed the horror of the morning to sink in. Amy had her knees on the ground, her fingers clawing at the dirt. Tears flowed from her eyes as she wailed. Ella was out of the tent before I could even gather my thoughts. Curious, the neighbors on the other side of us poked their heads out of their tent. Mom raced to me and pulled me outside.

"W-what's– ," I began.

"It's Margot." Mom interrupted before my question was finished. "She's gone."

•   •   •   •   •

Policemen swarmed the area within minutes, questioning us immediately. Already, officers and their scent dogs were scouring the Thicket and campgrounds for any traces of Margot. Larry was close enough for me to make out his words to one of the cops as he replayed what happened after Christian had disappeared.

"We all stayed up. It was about 3:20 a.m. I remember because Willow asked Nick what time it was before she and Ella went to bed. A few minutes after they left, Amy and Margot got into our own tent to sleep. Nick and Eve probably went to bed at, oh I don't know, 4 a.m.? And that's when I joined my wife and daughter."

"Okay, and what time did you last physically see Margot?" The officer asked.

Larry sighed. "When I got in the tent, she was sleeping on her own mattress. I settled in next to Amy and fell asleep pretty fast. We woke up at 6:15, and that's when we noticed she wasn't in the tent. When we realized she wasn't in the bathrooms or in the campsite, we called 911."

My heart sank as Larry's voice cracked. Mom had her arm around Amy, who was distraught as she told her version of events to a different cop, matching Larry's story almost word-for-word. I put my arm around Ella as she buried her head in my shoulder, tears staining my sweatshirt. The flashback entered my mind so quickly I couldn't shake it off.

"Mom! Mom!" Blades of grass sliced my legs as I ran desperately through the Thicket back to our campsite, Natalie's hand clasped tightly in mine. Behind me, Ella carried five-year-old Margot on her hip as she followed me. We flew into the campsite, dirt spraying behind us as I began to explain, words tumbling out of my mouth.

"Willow, slow down. What happened?" Mom's worried eyes met mine and I took a deep breath.

"Daniel was watching us from the parking lot. When we were in the forest. I ..." I took another breath, willing oxygen to enter my lungs.

"I think he was going to kidnap us."

"Kidnap you? Oh my gosh, what makes you say such a thing? Did he threaten you? Are you hurt?" Mom asked.

I stopped. "Well, no. But mom, he was watching us! It was weird and...uncomfortable. I think he would have tried to come get us if we hadn't run away. I don't even think Natalie is really his daughter and–"

My mother held up a hand and turned to Natalie, who was shaking like a leaf beside me. "Honey, I know you don't want to talk, but we need you to tell us. Is Daniel your dad?"

My mouth dropped to the floor as Natalie, at last, spoke to us.

"No."

Police sirens surrounded the campsite, though they weren't too loud for me. Just as several cops exited their vehicles, Daniel strode up to us. "What in the world is going on? Is Natalie okay?" He reached for the small child, but Mom shoved Natalie behind her legs.

"Don't you touch her," she instructed.

"That's my daughter, you bitch!" He shot back.

Daniel pushed Mom's shoulder, but a cop already had a grip on him and led him away for questioning.

An officer with short brown hair and a determined look on her face pulled Amy and Mom aside, while another cop tried talking to Natalie. After a few minutes of Ella, Margot, and me waiting patiently at the picnic table, I watched in astonishment as Natalie was returned to Daniel. I abruptly stood, opening my mouth to say something, when Mom and the brunette officer came over.

"Hi, sweetie. Do you mind telling me what made you think Daniel was going to harm you when you were in the woods?" I flinched from the cop's demeaning voice.

"He was watching us when we were playing in the trees. Isn't that weird? He dropped his daughter off but then stayed nearby to watch us."

The officer nodded her head, as if she understood what I felt. "I see how that's strange, but maybe he was worried about his daughter and wanted to keep an eye on her before he ran some errands," the cop suggested lightly.

"But Natalie just said--," I started to speak.

"Kids say things all the time that aren't true. Natalie is so young. We checked her over, and she is completely fine physically. We also did a background check on Daniel, and records state that he is her biological father."

I let the words sink in. How could that be true? I was so sure Daniel was up to something. The way he looked at us while we played in the trees...

"I am so sorry we bothered you with this. We'll talk to her about making assumptions. It won't happen again," my mother assured the cop as she strolled over to her police car. They spoke in hushed voices for a few minutes before all the police officers left the campsite.

Daniel and Natalie began walking away, hand-in-hand. Embarrassment flooded me. She was his daughter. I was so quick to think the worst of him.

"If it helps, I thought he was kind of weird, too." Ella patted my shoulder comfortingly.

"Willow," Dad's stern voice echoed in my ear. He gestured for me to come over to him and Mom. I sighed.

"Honey, I know you were concerned today. It was an odd situation."

I nodded, acknowledging what he was kind enough not to say, at least not yet. "I'm sorry."

"Okay, that's good. It's just, well, we accused a man of something really serious, and it turned out to be completely untrue. So, be careful about jumping to conclusions." I could nearly feel the embarrassment and shame rolling off my parents in waves.

I apologized again before plopping down in a camping chair and squeezing my eyes shut. I didn't want to cry in front of everyone. I blinked a couple times to clear my blurry vision, noticing that Daniel and Natalie were still strolling together back toward their campsite. As they reached the bend in the road, Daniel turned around. Even though he was a few campsites ahead, I could clearly make out his facial features.

Daniel gave me a sly smile and winked before turning back around and continuing to walk.

"Willow. Willow!" Mom shaking my shoulders snapped me out of my memory. "A policeman found one of Margot's shoes near the public access trail that leads to the beach."

I gasped, gripping her arm tightly. "Just her shoe? They haven't found her yet?"

Mom shook her head sadly. "One of the dogs picked up a scent though, and they're onto it now."

The feeling of déjà vu permeated my thoughts. I had been here and done this before. I had thought Daniel would kidnap us, that he had kidnapped Natalie. And I had been wrong. But now, Christian had likely kidnapped Margot.

My gut instinct was right this time.

The second I noticed Christian in his campsite when we had pulled up on Thursday, I felt deep down that something was off. I took a deep breath. Maybe it really was okay to trust myself again.

"What can we do to help?" I asked Mom.

Chaos consumed the campground. Police and their dogs still scoured the Thicket. Some campers nearby were packing up quickly to leave. I couldn't blame them. A child was missing, and no one felt safe anymore. It was selfish of me, but I wished the random campers would stay and help look for her.

"I was about to ask the same thing," Peyton's familiar voice called from behind me as she and Kyle strode into our campsite. My bottom lip quivered. At least *someone* was showing up for us.

Peyton enveloped me quickly in a hug. Kyle shook Larry's hand then Dad's. A petite woman with blonde, curly hair that resembled Peyton's stepped out from behind Kyle.

"I'm Lisa, Kyle's wife and Peyton's aunt. I am so sorry to hear what happened. What can we do to help find her?" The woman spoke softly, and I could immediately tell she was horrified at what had happened to Margot.

"The police are combing through the forest and heading down to the beach soon. If you want to hop in the search, by all means, do. We were told to stay here in case she comes back." Larry's voice was hoarse, emotion imbuing every word he spoke.

Kyle and Lisa nodded. Kyle placed his hand on Peyton's back, leading her toward the search. "Let's go, sugar," he whispered to her.

"We'll start by the trail where her shoe was found and ask the police where to go from there. We're happy to help." Lisa reached out and gripped Amy's shoulder. "They'll find her. I know it."

As the three turned around and walked toward the beach, a policewoman who had questioned us earlier jogged over.

"Hi, are all of you staying in these two campsites?" she gestured to the Grisham's site and ours, and Mom nodded.

"Listen, I know this is really tough on you. I need your help, *all* of you." The policewoman, whose name tag read "Cleo," trained her eyes specifically on Ella and me with her last words.

"Anything. We'll help with anything," Amy said, burying her face in Larry's shoulder.

"If your daughter somehow escaped this man, where would she go? We're trying to chase down every theory. If Margot was kidnapped, but managed to escape, we need to know where to look for her," Cleo said firmly. Her eyes roamed over each of us in assessment. Larry shook his head, explaining that Margot would likely just come back to the campsite, when I thought of something—Margot's words during flashlight tag when I suggested hiding in a new spot.

"Why don't we just hide in our first spot, under the bush? It's the best hiding spot!"

Ella, Margot, and I knew the flashlight tag area inside and out. We had been playing for years. I interrupted Larry and cleared my throat.

"I know a spot you should check."

CHAPTER 16

I led the way down the eerie path, since the police were not as familiar with the designated flashlight tag spot as Ella and I were. Larry and Amy stayed behind, as they were instructed to be at the campsite in case Margot escaped and came back. My parents filed in behind Ella and me as we, once again, trudged down the familiar path. It wasn't as haunting in the daytime, but the energy remained the same. Saturday night, the excitement had been tangible, buzzing as campers prepared to take part in the fun game. Now, it wasn't excitement that electrified the air, but hope.

Hope that Margot had somehow escaped Christian and hidden in the place where she knew he would never find her. Hidden in the place she knew best, the place we had never been caught.

Ella and I slowed our steps as we approached the wooden post jutting out of the sand. Base.

I blew out a breath and turned to my best friend.

"Are you ready?" I asked her quietly. She nodded.

I motioned to the handful of police officers behind my parents. "It's this way."

We silently marched to the right, following the sandy path lined with trees on one side and shrubs and dune grass on the other. The bramble bush that Ella, Margot, and I hollowed out years ago was now in front of us. In the light of day, it appeared like any other bush. The perfect hiding place.

I pointed underneath the thick tangle of branches.

"We cleared out a path underneath this bush a while ago. If you crawl under it, there's an opening inside the bush where we usually hide," I explained. Cleo crouched down and eyed the bush, frowning.

"Sergeant, there's no way any of us can fit under there. One of the girls is going to have to go in," she said.

The sergeant's eyebrows knitted together, and he whispered something to the officer next to him.

"Have the sister go in," he finally relented.

I squeezed Ella's shoulder in encouragement before she got onto her stomach and disappeared inside the bush. With bated breath, I listened as hard as I could, closing my eyes and desperately pleading that Margot had escaped and hidden here. I reminded myself gently that if Margot wasn't there, there were still tons of officers searching the beach for her.

"Ella!" It was the distinct voice of Margot.

A moment later, Ella emerged from the bush, sticks tangled in her hair, wiping tears from her eyes.

"She's in there." I could barely breathe as my best friend continued. "She escaped him, and she's in the bush. Please help her."

I threw my arms around Ella. Tears flowed down my cheeks as I held my best friend, Mom's loud sobbing echoing behind me. Police officers coaxed Margot out of the thorny bush, where she shakily stood up. Her dirty blonde hair hung messily out of her ponytail. Small scratches covered her hands and face. I couldn't take my eyes off her, barely allowing myself to believe she had escaped alive. As soon as her sister fully emerged, Ella gripped her in a tight hug, unwilling to let go.

"I'm sorry. Mom promised Christian wouldn't get to you, and he did, and I'm sorry." Ella's words were muffled as she apologized profusely to the small girl.

Cleo touched Ella's shoulder gently before saying, "I know you want to comfort Margot, but we need to question her. Christian is still out there, and we need to find him. We need the whole story."

Ella tearfully nodded, holding Margot's hand in hers protectively. Margot chewed on her bottom lip thoughtfully. Confused, I watched as the young girl tugged on Ella's sweatshirt.

"Yes, Margot?" Ella asked.

Margot's eyes darted back and forth between all the officers and her sister. She was struggling with how to say something, unsure of herself. Ella rubbed Margot's back soothingly. "It's okay, Christian can't get you now," she reassured her.

Margot shook her head, at last speaking the words she had been so clearly holding in for the last few seconds. "It wasn't Christian that took me."

A staticky voice came through an officer's radio before anyone answered Margot. The officer stepped to the side and returned the radio call, his voice too quiet for me to discern what he was saying. A few moments later, the officer placed his radio back on his belt and rejoined us.

"That was Officer Hart. They found him," he said calmly.

"Christian?" Cleo asked impatiently.

The officer's hand rested gently on his radio as he replied. "Not Christian. They found someone named Daniel."

CHAPTER 17

The Westport Police Department was surprisingly the nicest building in the whole shabby town. The fluorescent lights were bright but not blinding, and the air smelled of warm coffee and cinnamon. The only downside was the uncomfortable chairs in the waiting area, which was where my parents and I sat as Ella and Margot were in the interview room with their parents and an officer. I took a deep breath, knowing my turn was next.

When Margot recounted her story to us earlier, I was completely shell-shocked.

The girl who was like a sister to me had explained that sometime in the early morning, while everyone was at long last asleep, Margot had woken up. She had been thirsty and remembered that her water bottle was on the picnic table. By this time, it was about 5:45 a.m., so it was becoming light outside. Margot said she felt safe since it wasn't dark and decided to retrieve her water.

Once she ventured outside the tent, the man was ready. He had been lying in wait, observing. He was opportunistic, which made him even more dangerous.

Not Christian.

Daniel.

The Daniel we had stumbled upon three years ago. He grabbed Margot and dragged her through the Thicket, covering her mouth as she kicked and tried to scream. Margot told us that after a few minutes, she stopped fighting. It was exhausting, and she wanted to be ready to run away from him if she could. She said when they reached the public access trail, there were no beachgoers in the parking lot. She began to scream and kick again, which is when her shoe came off.

Daniel told her to stop making noise or he'd kill her, so Margot complied. It was around this time that Daniel received a phone call. When the police officer asked her who she thought it was on the other line, Margot shook her head.

"I don't know," she said, "but Daniel wasn't happy. I thought maybe whoever was on the phone was trying to meet us on the beach or something."

Margot had gone on, saying once they reached the beach, a man and woman were strolling down by the water. Daniel froze when he saw them, clearly unnerved that someone could catch him with a stolen child.

Once Margot noticed he was caught off-guard, she took her chance to run. She kicked Daniel as hard as she could in the leg, praying it would slow him down enough for her to get away. Then she said her body automatically took off in the direction of our hiding spot, almost out of habit. As soon as she reached it, she tucked herself away, just like we had during flashlight tag.

At the police station, the detectives were questioning Margot again, recording every detail. Since she was a minor, Larry and Amy had to be present. I assumed Daniel was somewhere secure, hopefully being interrogated. I bounced my knee up and down, wondering when they would call me and my parents in. The police wanted to know about the incident with Daniel and Natalie from three years ago.

All that Mom had gleaned so far from an officer was that Daniel was a registered sex offender from Louisiana. Since learning this information and arriving at the station, my parents had been quiet.

Mom placed a hand on my knee, quelling the repetitive movement.

"Willow," she said softly. I turned my head away from her. "Willow, I'm so sorry. We were wrong this whole time about Daniel."

My mother's words smacked me right in the gut. I expected to feel some sort of "I told you so" notion of triumph, but as I met Mom's red-rimmed eyes, I felt the opposite. I could sense her regret. How could any of us have known he would come back years later and kidnap Margot? Even though I sensed something off with Daniel and Natalie, I never truly believed he'd go as far as he did today.

"It's okay. The police told you Natalie was his daughter. What could you have done?" I said, meeting their guilt-ridden faces and working to project calmness in my voice.

"We could have believed you anyway. You explicitly told us you thought something was strange about Daniel. We are so, so sorry, honey. Your father and I didn't even take your feelings about Christian seriously either, and look what he ended up doing," Mom continued.

I paused. "Wait, where is Christian? Did they ever find him?"

Dad shook his head in defeat. "No. It doesn't sit right with me, even if Christian didn't 'break' the law. He's still a sketchy character."

"Excuse me, Willow Carter? We'd like to speak with you now," a woman dressed in a fitted suit spoke gently, holding a file and motioning for me to follow her. My parents walked beside me. I was also a minor, so they had to be present anyway. We were led to a well-lit interview room with one table in the middle. The woman in the power suit motioned for us to sit down before she exited the room. I took a seat, one parent on each side of me, pleased to see it was Cleo settled across from me. I felt comfortable talking with her.

Cleo patted the stack of files in front of her and placed her glasses on her nose. "Let's start at the beginning."

•   •   •   •   •

As my parents and I recapped the incident with Daniel and Natalie a few years ago, Cleo wrote feverishly in her notepad.

"But the police told us Natalie was Daniel's daughter and there were no charges against him. As far as we knew, he and Natalie left that same day after the police were gone." Mom finished her statement, folding her hands neatly on her lap. Cleo lifted her pen and stared down at her notes.

"Thank you for coming in and talking to us. I don't think we need anything else from you right now. You're free to go back to your campsite. Daniel is being questioned, and we have men looking for Christian as we speak." Her warm smile was reassuring.

The Grishams met us back at the campgrounds later that afternoon. We reconvened at the picnic table, where we recounted the events of the day in disbelief.

"You know, I'm still unnerved that Christian is out there somewhere. All his stuff is still right there." Amy sighed, pointing to the abandoned campsite next to us. The blue Coleman tent and matching camp chair were in the same position they'd been in when we arrived on Thursday. Christian's car was still parked in front of his tent, making the scene even more sinister. It appeared...deserted.

"Maybe we should leave tonight instead of tomorrow?" Mom lightly suggested.

Larry quickly shook his head. "I don't have it in me to drive all the way back to Idaho today. I'm exhausted, honestly."

All of us murmured our agreement.

"Are we still allowed to play in the Thicket?" Margot asked Amy.

Amy gave her a stern look. "Absolutely not. Stay close by. Christian is still out there, and we want you to be safe." Her instruction was firm but laced with protectiveness and love. Margot's shoulders drooped.

"How about we play some cribbage until dinner? I bet you can beat me," I poked her in the side, hoping to get her mind off everything.

"What about three-way cribbage?" Ella said. "That way we can see who the best cribbage player is between us."

Margot giggled and agreed. The three of us played through dinner and until night fell across the campground. It was a temporary distraction for what we knew was inevitable—going to bed. Even though our dads were going to take turns watching the campsite overnight, a tangible feeling of uneasiness spread throughout everyone. One little pull and we would all come undone.

The three of us cleaned up the cribbage game, placing the pegs back into the board and filing away the cards. Ella's head suddenly whipped around toward Mom, who was putting away dry dishes into her camp kitchen.

"What?" I probed her.

"Oh, sorry. You probably didn't hear. Your mom's phone is ringing," she said.

Mom muttered a few words into the phone before putting it on speaker, gesturing for everyone to gather around her to listen.

"Okay, detective, I have you on speaker. I don't know how long the call will last before getting dropped. The service is horrible out here," she said.

"Where are you guys?" I immediately recognized Cleo's voice on the other end of the line, and it was filled with tension.

Larry frowned, suspicion lining his face. "We're at our campsite. Why?"

"Listen to me. Is anyone else there next to you, other than you guys?" Cleo's voice sounded worried.

Mom shot Dad a concerned look before saying, "Nope, just us and the kids. Why?"

Cleo paused. Her voice was becoming glitchy, but we all heard her when she finally said, "Do you know a Kyle Moynes?"

CHAPTER 18

I couldn't breathe. My eyes were locked with Ella's, who stood across from me now while Mom placed herself in the center of everyone, phone in hand. Nobody answered Cleo for what felt like an eternity.

"Yes, w-we know Kyle. He's here every year and leads flashlight tag for all the kids." Dad's powerful voice was shaking.

"Listen, don't go near him. We found out he's–" Cleo's statement was cut short as the call dropped. Mom groaned, trying to call her back immediately. The adults all promptly put their heads together and whispered.

Thick fog had settled over the campground. Everyone's voices around me suddenly became drowned out, a mere echo in the recesses of my mind as my wild thoughts consumed me. I thought back to the night of flashlight tag, when I had realized something about Christian nagged at me that I couldn't place. He seemed familiar to me. Desperate, I replayed the unsettling incident in my head, trying to analyze what it was about Christian's features that stood out to me.

It came to me so fast, I felt like I was knocked backwards.

It wasn't something about Christian's *features* that was familiar. It was part of his vocabulary. When he was coaxing us to come with him since he had "caught" us, he had called me a nickname. His words echoed in my head.

"Come on, sugar."

Years ago, when Daniel had dropped Natalie off.

"See you later, sugar."

Goosebumps ran up my arms, prickling the back of my neck. Something was still bothering me. Why was Cleo asking if we knew Kyle? Kyle, the handsome, trusted firefighter. Peyton's uncle, the leader of our treasured flashlight tag. He had just helped search for

...

The goosebumps were nothing compared to the deep-boned chill that devoured my entire body when I realized what was niggling at the back of my mind.

The search.

Kyle had gently nudged Peyton.

"Let's go, sugar."

I gasped, covering my mouth with my hand. Mom immediately strode toward me, giving up on calling Cleo back.

"Willow, what's wrong?"

A sudden rustle startled all of us. Coach's ears perked up, my only signal where the noise was coming from. The seven of us cautiously followed Coach's gaze, which was fixed on Christian's car. Another noise resounded from behind the vehicle, and I saw Margot flinch out of the corner of my eye.

Did Christian come back for his car?

"You better show yourself, Christian! Get your scrawny ass out here and face us!" Larry yelled. I glanced at his ankle, which still held his pistol.

A figure emerged from behind the car, hands in the air. Through the dense, gray fog, it was hard to make out who it was. The person stepped closer, and swept back into so many happy memories in this campground, I found myself breathing a short sigh of relief.

Kyle!

Oh no. Kyle.

Alarm bells rang in my head. Ah, there it was again—the gut instinct like when I first noticed Christian.

Except now, I was getting that feeling for the very first time from a man I knew. A man I had trusted.

The tension in the air was palpable. Unsaid words hung between us like prey dangling in front of a predator. Everyone had their guard up, unsure of what Kyle was involved in.

Or if he was even involved. If we hadn't lost service, Cleo would have been able to explain more.

"Sorry, I didn't mean to startle you. I think I dropped my phone near here earlier and just stopped by to look for it." Kyle calmly lowered his hands.

Larry surveyed Kyle warily, his gaze darting back and forth between the firefighter and all of us. Kyle's cerulean eyes were uncannily bright in the darkness.

Coach swiveled his head toward Mom. She was close enough to me now that my good ear picked up the sound this time.

Her phone was ringing.

Mom's eyes flashed to the device on the picnic table just a couple feet away.

"Don't you want to answer that?" Kyle's husky tone now exuded a hint of arrogance as he challenged my mother.

Mom reached for her phone and slid her finger across it, holding it to her ear. I hopelessly listened to her side of the conversation, Cleo's voice much too quiet for anyone to hear. Mom nodded.

"Yes."

Another pause while Cleo answered her.

"Mhmm. I see."

I realized I was holding my breath, so I released a shaky exhale. Kyle's eyes were trained on Mom as she finally said, "Thank you," and hung up the phone.

"You know, don't you?" Kyle chuckled as he spoke. He leaned against Christian's car casually, crossing one leg over the other.

We didn't know what Kyle was talking about, really, but he didn't know that.

"Know what?" Dad finally said.

Kyle gave Mom a sly smile. "Did you figure it all out? Detective filled you in?"

Mom simply nodded, appearing unshaken by the phone call and by Kyle. She gave Dad a look I couldn't decipher then shoved her hands in her pockets.

"Cleo filled me in, but I want to hear it from you. Apparently, you're some mastermind, so please, I'm sure you'd like to brag about yourself to us," my mother said, confronting Kyle. The same thought I had spoken out loud days ago about Christian resounded through my head again.

What can he do, when there are seven of us and one of him?

"Girls, go to the car," Amy ordered. She lifted her hand to toss the car keys to Ella when Kyle held his hand up in protest. This time, he clenched a shiny, dark object. I swallowed, trying to crush the panic crawling up my throat.

It was a gun.

"Don't. The girls deserve to hear this, as they were the original victims, anyway," Kyle said. He briefly lowered the gun, aiming it at the ground.

"We have weapons too, you know. There's only one of you and several of us," Dad said, challenging him.

Right as Kyle smiled, I felt something sharp poke into my back. I went rigid and whispered, "Mom."

Everyone turned to me, their eyes widening in terror as they registered why Kyle was so confident we would cooperate with him. I didn't have to face him to know. Christian was behind me, his breath stale in my ear as he grabbed me and positioned the knife above my throat.

"If any of you move, Christian slits Willow's throat," Kyle said. Tears clouded my eyes as Christian's grip tightened around me as he isolated me from everyone, dragging me a few feet backwards. Coach was growling furiously at the end of his lead, helplessly connected to the metal leg of the picnic table. Margot whimpered, and Kyle swung the gun at her quickly.

"Don't make a sound. We're going to tell you what to do. First, you're going to have Margot walk toward me. If I see one of you even flinch, Christian will kill Willow and take Ella instead."

I couldn't believe other campers weren't awake or nearby to see this.

"Hey, you told me I'd get the woman," Christian yelled to Kyle from behind me, tightening his grasp.

"The reason we're in this situation in the first place is because you couldn't resist your own urges and tried to get into her pants with her husband right there!" Kyle bellowed, anger seeping from his voice. "That wasn't the plan!"

"Just because you and Daniel prefer innocent kids doesn't mean I do," Christian said, seething. "I told you I didn't even know if I wanted to be part of this!

Taking kids for yourself is one thing, but selling them? That's a whole different ball game." Christian's words felt like a faint echo in my ears. It suddenly all made sense.

Kyle's family camped here the same weekend as us every year. He had clearly been scouting out kids over the years for Daniel, and possibly himself. Natalie probably was a lure to get us out into the Thicket so he could take us. It hadn't worked, and Daniel's plan was nearly uncovered when we called the police. They waited a couple years so as not to look suspicious then added Christian into the strategy, since we wouldn't recognize him.

Kyle must have told Christian we would be at flashlight tag, and that's how he knew where to find us. All these years, Kyle and Daniel had been plotting to abduct us. And who knew how many other innocent girls had been taken by them at other places and other times. My panic subsided for a brief moment, replaced with something else.

Anger.

I loved Westport. I loved camping here and playing out in the Thicket. I enjoyed the beach days and flashlight tag. This whole time, a monster had lurked in the corners, watching my every move. He had strategized, patiently waiting for the perfect moment to capture my best friends and me and use us in whatever sick way he wanted.

Kyle strode forward, irritation oozing out of him, fixating only on Christian.

At that moment, he forgot.

He forgot there were seven of us, and one of him.

He angrily stomped past Larry, heading straight for Christian and me. Larry grabbed the pistol from his holster in one split second and raised it at Kyle.

"Kyle, look out!" Christian cried out. The burly firefighter turned on Larry, gun ready, but he was too slow. Larry fired, hitting Kyle in the thigh.

Kyle went down with a yelp of pain. I took my chance, just as Margot had with Daniel, and elbowed Christian in the gut. I sprinted to our car, Christian right on my heels. Swinging the door open, I dug inside the center console until cold steel touched my fingertips.

Christian dove for me, and I whipped around, Dad's gun in my hands.

It was a really good thing I had taken that class on gun safety last summer.

His eyes widened, but he covered it with a sneer. "You won't actually shoot me. I know that."

This time, I smiled back at him. "I won't have to."

Ella released Coach from his lead, and the herding dog came barreling over. His jaw clamped down tightly around Christian's right ankle, immediately causing the man to crumple to the ground. I'd forgotten there were eight of us, not just seven. Coach shook his head back and forth with Christian's lower leg still in his mouth, unwilling to let go even though the man was screaming in pain. Dad raced over, scooping up the discarded knife before Christian could get a hold of it again.

"It's okay, Coach," I gasped for air.

Coach's eyes darted to me, and he reluctantly let go of Christian's leg, leaving him sprawled out on the ground with blood seeping through his pants.

Dad embraced me, shoving my face against his sweaty chest. "How did you know the gun was in there?" he asked through his tears of relief.

I pulled back enough to meet his eyes. "I saw the look you and mom gave each other earlier. It took me a second, but I realized I couldn't see the gun in your waistband. Also ..." I grinned at him before finishing, "It was kind of a gut instinct."

Two Years Later

I paced anxiously in front of the Ford Expedition, my feet nearly wearing a hole in the soft dirt.

"Willow, pacing won't make time go by any faster!" Mom called out from under the EZ-Up. I chuckled and checked my phone again. No new messages.

"Help me set up the tent, will you, Eve?" Dad poked Mom in the side playfully. Swatting him with the kitchen towel, she began running around the picnic table, Dad chasing her. He finally picked her up and swung her around, laughing as their bodies became entangled. Happiness swelled in my chest. They had been doing so much better for the last two years. Therapy had definitely helped all of us, and my parents had committed to putting in the tough work for their relationship. All the marital counseling, classes, and honest conversations were paying off. Dad was now a year and a half sober, and Mom supported him every step of the way.

A small, white butterfly fluttered by me, circling my head a few times before landing on my purple and gold sweatshirt. I had chosen the University of Washington for their strong biology program, hoping it would propel me forward in my desired career field of animal care. The butterfly moved slowly across my embroidered college sweatshirt before flying off. I lifted my hair into a ponytail as the sun shone down onto our campsite, filtering in beautifully through the trees. As I gathered my hair up, my finger brushed against the medical device that was now positioned above my deaf ear. I was still getting used to the cochlear implant, but I was grateful we could afford such an expensive device. It helped me immensely in the big lecture classes at the University of Washington.

A car rumbled in the distance, a sound I could now hear clearly. Excitement tingled through my veins as the car drew closer, eventually parking in the next campsite over.

"Late again?" I shouted as the back door of the vehicle swung open.

"You should know us well enough by now!" Ella's sing-song voice filled the air. I sprinted toward her, embracing both her and Margot in a tight hug. Amy and Larry jumped out of the vehicle, greeting my parents warmly.

•   •   •   •   •

After Christian and Kyle were arrested that night two years before, the police had filled us in on the details of the investigation. Cleo had called Mom to inform her that detectives had uncovered Christian, Kyle, and Daniel's plan to begin a child prostitution ring. During the end of the call that night, Cleo had instructed Mom to stay put because officers were on their way. The officers had rolled up to our campsite just moments after Coach had bitten Christian again.

And Kyle and Daniel? They're brothers. Christian is their cousin, who they roped into their plans that year to attempt to kidnap us. It turns out Daniel had a vendetta against us for nearly ruining his operation years before.

The police officers figured out the three of them had committed offenses against several children already. Kyle had been befriending families at the campground for years, finding out personal information he and Daniel could use later to kidnap children out of their homes. Consequently, the three men were now sitting in jail for the rest of their lives.

The officers also found Natalie, who truly was Daniel's biological daughter, living with her mom. Somehow, she had gotten away from Daniel after that camping incident, and she and her mother had been on the run from him ever since. I was so relieved they could live their daily lives safely now that he was behind bars.

Neither my family nor the Grishams could find it in us to return to Westport the year after the horrifying experience with Christian, Kyle, and Daniel. We all carried trauma from that night, and Ella's life and mine were getting busier with college. Funnily enough, Dad told everyone that was the first year he had ever brought a gun while we camped in Westport. While he had been getting the car ready to go, he suddenly had a hunch to bring the gun, so he grabbed it just in case. He trusted his gut.

When Ella called a few months ago and asked if we would be willing to camp this year, my family had agreed after some deliberation. We loved this place and didn't want bad occurrences to tarnish our memories.

Ella and Margot released our hug, their grins wide and eyes twinkling as we pulled apart. "I can't believe it's been two years since I saw you. And two years since we were here!" Ella exclaimed.

Margot, now ten, appeared to have grown a foot, her dirty blonde hair reaching past her shoulders.

"You look grown up," I said, tucking a stray hair behind her ear.

"Is that who I think it is?" A voice I had heard many times before caused me to turn my head. Peyton stood on the outskirts of our campsite, her arms folded and a smile on her face.

As she walked closer, her grin faded, words tumbling out of her mouth. "Listen, my parents and I had *no* idea about Kyle, we—"

I clutched Peyton's hand in mine. "Peyton, we know. It's okay. It's not your fault he was a bad person," I consoled her gently. She nodded gratefully.

"Mom! Can we go into the Thicket?" Margot ran up to Amy, her eyes big and pleading, just as they had been two years ago. Amy ruffled her daughter's hair lovingly. She looked up at Ella, Peyton, and me before returning her gaze to her youngest.

"Yes. But be careful. And take Coach," she said calmly. Margot threw her arms around her mother before running back to join us. The three of us began traipsing into the trees when Peyton spoke hesitantly from behind us. "Do you mind if I join?"

I motioned with my arm for her to follow us. "Are you kidding me? The more, the merrier. Come on!"

The four of us ventured back out into the Thicket, the dense layers of trees surrounding us as we placed one foot in front of another. Coach panted happily behind us, following along. The grass still sliced my knees, and the woven treetops still blocked out much of the sunlight, allowing only tiny slivers to filter through.

"We're about to show you our legendary tree that we claimed years ago!" Margot told Peyton excitedly.

Soon, it came into view. The tree was covered in its usual soft, spongy moss, making it appear nearly all green with just bits of brown bark jutting out. A starling flew overhead, and I watched intently as it landed nearby in a nest. The tops of three oval eggs were poking out of it.

As Ella, Margot, and I settled into our usual positions on the tree, Peyton chose her own spot. Coach laid down at the base of the trunk, forever watching out for us, protecting us. The four of us dangled our feet in the air, the breeze swaying our hair lightly. The forest was quiet, as if it had been waiting for us all this time, waiting for us to come back and speak our secrets again, bare our souls, lay down our skeletons.

It felt like we had never left.

THE END

AUTHOR ACKNOWLEDGMENTS

I would first and foremost like to thank Suzanne Akerman, who was the first person to lay eyes on my work and do some amazing editing. Without her, I wouldn't have had the confidence in myself or my writing. I cannot thank her enough for the determination she instilled in me and for all the help she gave me through long hours of editing. I would also like to thank my husband, Alec McNamara, for being there for all the late-night writing frustration. He handled everything with such compassion and grace, and I couldn't ask for a more supportive partner. To my parents, I'd like to thank them for encouraging me early on to write my heart out. I can't wait for them to read my words in the form of an actual book. Lastly, I would like to acknowledge Mary Ellen Bramwell, who is my official editor for this work. From our first phone call, I knew she would elevate my manuscript to a whole other level, and she did not disappoint.

ABOUT THE AUTHOR

Photo courtesy of Dawne Carlisle

Hannah McNamara is a zookeeper by day and a writer by night. After obtaining her B.A. in biology, Hannah pursued her passion of taking care of animals by earning a job at an accredited zoo but never gave up her love of writing. She loosely based *Gut Instinct* on a true story that happened to her family years ago while camping. Hannah lives in the beautiful Pacific Northwest with her husband and their three dogs and two cats. She always finds companionship in her hearing alert dog, Hopper, and loves to cuddle up with her while she writes. Follow Hannah on X @HannahMacWriter.

NOTE FROM
HANNAH MCNAMARA

Word-of-mouth is crucial for any author to succeed. If you enjoyed *Gut Instinct*, please leave a review online—anywhere you are able. Even if it's just a sentence or two. It would make all the difference and would be very much appreciated.

Thanks!
Hannah McNamara

We hope you enjoyed reading this title from:

www.blackrosewriting.com

Subscribe to our mailing list – *The Rosevine* – and receive
FREE books, daily deals, and stay current with news about
upcoming releases and our hottest authors.
Scan the QR code below to sign up.

Already a subscriber? Please accept a sincere thank you for
being a fan of Black Rose Writing authors.

View other Black Rose Writing titles at
www.blackrosewriting.com/books
and use promo code
PRINT to receive a **20% discount** when purchasing.